TIME AND SPACE BETWEEN US

DIANA KNIGHTLEY

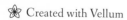

For Kevin, I would, yes...

CHAPTER 1

$\mathcal{I}$ was still licking the hunks of chocolate lava cake off my fingers from our dessert when Magnus, sitting on one of the kitchen stools, took my hand and pulled me closer between his legs.

It was still a little awkward to kiss him. There weren't a lot of places on his body that weren't painfully injured. I couldn't touch him without causing him to wince.

"Are you feeling better?" I pressed closer, keeping my hands on his thighs, off his back.

"Och aye." He ran his hands up the back of my thighs to my panties. He pulled my hips closer.

"Would you like your massage?"

In answer he led me to our room, our bed.

I helped him peel his shirt off his back, not easy with so many bandages. Then I dropped his kilt to the ground and took a deep breath to steady myself.

I missed him. I wanted him. It had been way too long.

As he crawled to the middle of our bed, I pulled my shirt off, unfastened my bra, and slid it down my arms.

He dropped face down on the bed, but turned in time to see me shimmy my shorts and panties down. His eyes went wide.

A smile spread across his mouth. "You are disrobed mo reul-iuil, tis markedly different from yesterday's massage."

I poured a dollop of oil into the palm of my hand, grinned, and climbed astride his lower back. I massaged across the top of his wide shoulders. The whip marks there weren't as deep. I pressed down the side of his arms. Up and down, pressing and pulling. Wherever I could touch where the skin wasn't marred. He moaned happily as I burrowed my fingers into a tightly bound muscle and spasmed when I accidentally grazed an especially angry looking wound. "I'm sorry."

"Nae matter, Kaitlyn. Tis painful, but I feel clear for the first time in days, turadh."

I pressed my hands along his left tricep. "Remind me what that means?"

He groaned with pleasure. "Turadh, the clouds have broken."

"Oh. God, I love it when you say things like that — in Gaelic, right?" I pressed my palms to his triceps and wiggled my hips on his back.

He growled and rose up, bucking.

I squealed as I slid off his slippery back to the bed.

"Tha thu breagha." He pinned my wrists and climbed on my body. "Is ann leatsa abhios mo chridhe gubrath."

"Oh my god, Magnus, that is fucking hot."

"Mo reul-iuil..." He shoved hard and fast up into me, desperate and intense, holding my arms above my head, his mouth pressed to my neck. My moans started low but grew as he rocked and pushed against me. His body had been sitting idle and broken, but now strong and powerful. His forehead butted against my cheek; his breath filled my ear. "You art mo reul-iuil."

"Oh — oh — oh my god," I arched against him with a moan as waves rolled through me. He held on, riding, his voice a groan. It rumbled up from his chest as he finished and collapsed on my body.

We both lay still. Panting. Slowly catching our breaths. Kissing the spots of skin closest to our mouths. I wriggled my wrists free from his grip and clasped around his hands. I kissed and nibbled his neck.

Then he kissed me, slow. His tongue flicked around my teeth, teasing my lips.

We stared into each other's eyes.

"I missed you so much."

"Och aye." He kissed my lips, the tip of my nose, my chin. "I can tell ye have been wanting me, ye are talking to God." He chuckled, kissed my neck, and rolled off me to his side.

I curled up beside him. His strong hand on my hip.

I loved him more than I ever believed possible, but the last thing he said just before he fell asleep was, "I would bide here forever if I could."

I knew in my heart that loving him wasn't enough to convince him to stay.

CHAPTER 2

*T*he next morning Magnus was sitting on a deck chair, leaned forward, elbow on his knees, making imaginary marks on the thin layer of sand between his feet. Quentin, now his number one security guard, was nodding, listening, occasionally asking a question.

Magnus was leaving.

I knew it because of what he said when I talked to him about the estate while he was still in the hospital: "Tis good Kaitlyn, how ye have caused it to grow, verra good." His words were proud. As if he was a parent watching a child start out in a life they couldn't really share in. He was watching me grow our estate, not for us, but for me, alone.

He told me again that he was leaving soon. I begged him to stay. We ended the conversation with an uncomfortable agreement — there was no way to agree, so we wouldn't talk about it anymore.

So I had no idea what his plans were and that sucked.

But I couldn't imagine how to start the conversation. And I was frankly scared to. As if asking would make it real. Ignoring it would keep it improbable. But I needed to know, needed to get it out into the open.

I had to talk to him.

To beg him to stay.

So I planned, plotted, and carefully deliberated, and decided to bring it up in the office, in a dignified adult way.

But I forgot or disregarded all that planning and brought it up right after making love. In the middle of the night with silent tears rolling down my cheeks, already distraught. Childlike, wrapped in his arms, tears pooling on his chest. "Please don't go."

"What's this then?"

I clutched his shoulders, being mindful of his wounds. They were jagged, red, a few still open and sore. He told me the whip marks didn't hurt that much, that he could lay on his back, that I didn't need to be gentle. But his back looked so angry, painful, and deeply, deeply wounded that I felt like it was a reminder why it was too dangerous for him to return to Scotland. He couldn't see it. Maybe that was why he was so determined to go.

"You're leaving and you don't have to... you don't."

"Ah, Kaitlyn, ye know... we have discussed this—"

"We haven't, we haven't discussed it. Not enough. I don't know why. Not really. And you're making the plans without me, and it's just like with my—"

He shifted his head and his hand that had been stroking my shoulder paused.

"What are ye saying?"

I sobbed. "That just like everyone else, you're leaving me and lying to me about it and — am I not worth staying for?"

Magnus huffed. He tensed, then rolled out from under me, and sat on the edge of the bed. His bandaged back turned to me. He sat there for a moment, facing the wall of windows. Very quietly.

Panic hit me in the gut. He had turned his back on me.

He said, "Tis nae fair."

"What isn't fair?" I reached for his hand.

He pulled it away and rubbed it across his thigh.

"You are saying this tae me? Comparing me tae your other men, Kaitlyn? I am your husband. I will nae stand for this."

I was too shocked to know what to say. In my imagination this went so much better.

"I know, I just—"

"You are my wife. When I tell ye I must away, you should say goodbye without a fuss. And I'll have nae more of speakin' of other men in my bed."

"I'm sorry I brought up my past. I only wanted you to know one of the reasons why this was too hard for me. I'm sorry."

His jaw clenched. "In the future, here, know ye one thought, your husband, Magnus Archibald Caehlin Campbell has been true tae ye."

I curled up around my knees wishing I could sink away. My voice was so small it shocked me when I spoke. "It doesn't feel like truth, it feels like a lie of omission. Just because you don't lie out loud doesn't make it not a lie. There's a truth you're refusing to say." I looked up at his back.

His face turned to mine. His eyes glaring dark. "You call me a liar?"

"You aren't telling me the truth. From here, in the pit of my stomach, and here in my heart, it feels very much the same."

He turned to the windows again. I squirmed up to the pillow, taking a view of the side of his face. His jaw clenched and unclenched. I had hoped that starting this conversation might be an immediate relief, but no, I felt really terrible and desperate. He was headed out the door and my hand was on his back shoving him through.

"You are a woman, ye will try tae convince me tae stay. You canna understand why I must fight. You see my wounds and want tae heal me, and ye want me tae hide here. Just as Lady Mairead—"

"If we're not to talk of men in your bed, I would appreciate not comparing me to your mother in mine."

Magnus let out an appreciative chuckle. Then shook his head.

I continued, "I do want to convince you to stay. Explain to me why I can't. I'm listening. If you'll listen to me."

His head hung. "I daena want tae leave ye. I canna talk of it without changin' my mind, and I must nae change my mind. You want me tae listen tae ye, you plan tae beg me tae stay, but ye do, every moment." He reached behind to take my hand, wrapping it in his. "Your smile begs me. Your body, your laugh, ye dinna need words, Kaitlyn. I am nae strong enough tae hear them."

"Then stay."

"I canna."

"Then tell me why."

And so he did. Sitting on the edge of the bed, lit by moonlight shimmering on his darkness. He exposed his shadows. He told me about his home, or lack of a home, in Scotland, the cusp of the eighteenth century. He had spent his youth at Balloch Castle, but when he was nine years old he had been sent to London to live with an uncle. He had been to court. Had lived and played with royals. But he had always been one of "the Highlanders," not fully trusted, not really fitting in.

Then his Uncle Baldie sent for him because Lady Mairead was missing, abducted. Suddenly, after growing up in a life of wealth and civilities, Magnus was thrust into danger and intrigues. "I lived at Balloch again. I trained to fight alongside my brother, with my cousins, but winna fully trusted for many reasons: My father was a foreigner. I grew up in London. I was Protestant. And maybe worse — the son of Lady Mairead. Twas a blight on my reputation."

"That must have been really hard."

"I dinna think on it much, there were feuds to fight." He gave me a small half-grin.

I squinted my eyes. "You like fighting?"

His eyes twinkled. "Tis hard to like something that may end me, but I am verra good at it. And is braw tae fight alongside my brother. There are troubles brewin' though. My clan is split in their minds and hearts. The next fight will be cousin against cousin. Up tae now I have been in the middle. They believe I am on both sides and nocht at all. Tis difficult tae prove my allegiance and is harder still tae prove my independence. But I must always be provin' m'self tae stay alive."

"Your own cousins are a danger to you?"

"Och aye, I have a great many cousins. Some are like brothers. Some are dangerous. A few are villainous."

"I have three cousins, they live in Alabama. I don't see them much."

"Tis good if they are villainous," he joked.

His face grew serious again. "I was sent to search for her in France, until finally Lady Mairead was found, in a castle in Scotland, married to Lord Delapointe. She sent for me. She made me take a binding oath tae follow her commands. Then she asked me tae recover one of these vessels from its hiding place and bring it tae her.

"I did as she asked, but when I returned with it, Lord Delapointe met me at the gates and fought me for it. Twas my first indication that the vessel was very valuable."

"That's awful."

"It was, in the ensuin' battle I killed John Baldrick, the brother of Delapointe."

"His brother?" My eyes were wide. "Have you killed many people?"

"Enough that we shoudna speak of it." He looked down at his

hands. "Lady Mairead met me on the field of battle tae take the vessel. As her hand clasped around it she spoke a numerical incantation. I was fearful and begged her nae tae perform spells, but she continued, and I was dragged here tae Fernandina Beach, the year 2017."

"You must have been terrified. That night you met James, you didn't know where you were or anything about the world you were in..."

"Twas terrible. But then I met ye, and you introduced me tae coffee, and after that twas all okay." He chuckled. "The truth is I am used tae being in places that are nae mine. I haena had a home in many years. I daena fit any—"

I pulled his hand to my heart. "This is your home Magnus. You belong here. You are my husband. This is true. I know it." I smiled. "I know it here." I drew his hand down between my legs. "And here."

He groaned happily. "I would live there if I could." He drew his hand away and turned back to the windows.

"Thank you for telling me. But it all sounds so complicated and dangerous; I still don't know why you have to go back."

"That is why I am nae talkin' tae ye about it."

"So what do you want me to say?"

"Kaitlyn, I want ye tae say, 'Aye master, I will do as ye wish,' and be done with it."

I flicked the sheets, pissed. "You're kidding me right? I have never in my life said anything like that to any man, and I'm not going to start now." I lay fuming. "I mean you've met me right? I'm Kaitlyn Sheffield, and I don't just take orders—"

"Your name is Kaitlyn Campbell, and ye will take orders from me—"

"No I won't."

"Let me finish. I would say — you will take orders from me as my wife, but as your husband I winna give them. Nae like that."

He scrubbed his palms down his face. "I knew what kind of woman ye are when I married ye. I knew Kaitlyn Campbell dinna take orders. Lady Mairead warned me. She said ye winna be a woman under my control, and I said that was good. I like ye with the fire in your throat and passion in your heart, but you asked what I want ye tae say and I answered — I want ye tae submit tae me. I know ye won't, so instead tis better nae tae talk of it."

"I want you to be able to talk to me about anything."

"I canna trust that ye will listen and nae beg me tae stay."

I huffed, threw the covers off my legs, swung my feet to the opposite side of the bed, and stood. "So you don't trust me and I don't trust you. That's a fine piece of horseshit of a marriage." I stomped into our bathroom and wanted to slam the door, but guess what, frosted, sliding glass. So I crossed my arms and pouted like a big baby for a few moments and then stomped back into the room.

He hadn't moved. He was still sitting, staring at his hands between his knees. The skin on his back cut and injured, his head hanging down.

And I softened.

Oh. "What do you need me to do?"

"I need tae talk tae ye about it. I need your help with something — tae be able tae trust ye tae help me go."

"Oh god Magnus, I'm so sorry." I dropped to my knees in front of him and clutched his hands. "You can trust me. I'll just — I can just listen. I will. Tell me." I laid my forehead on his hands and tried, really hard, to listen through my breaking heart.

"Delapointe wants all the vessels. If he finds them all it will make him verra powerful. There are three; he knows I have one. Lady Mairead still has one. The other is in his hands. Ye have seen the cuts on Lady Mairead's cheeks. He will torture her if he is given the chance.

"Also, I have killed his brother. He swore tae kill me, but he dinna. Instead he kept me locked and bound and beat me — he drove me close tae death. He only allowed me tae live as bait so Lady Mairead would come tae him."

"He knows I have one of the vessels and I have used it tae escape. He will follow me here. Then he will kill me. But he may wish to see me suffer first. And if he discovers you... I canna allow that tae happen. And that is the story of it — why I must go. Because living here is nae the end of it."

I looked up at him. "It sounds like you have to."

"I do Kaitlyn." He smiled sadly. "I must." He shook his head. "Our marriage is nae horseshit."

"Yeah. I know. I say stupid things sometimes. I'm trying to be better. To listen more."

He swept his arms around my back and pulled me up onto him, leaning back on the bed, me on top. He put his arms behind his head and I sat on his waist looking down. I loved this view: his bicep close to his ear, his shoulders bound with muscles, his chest wide. His eyes were appreciative, but he couldn't look on me for long, instead he focused on my thigh, my hips, kept his eyes cast down.

I asked him once, from this position above him, what he saw when he looked up at me — he answered, "An emanating light bursts from your skin. I must take ye in pieces, else I might cry." Then he chuckled.

I considered it a joke. But also a little bit true. He often mentioned how much light I emanated, which might have been the corniest compliment in the world if not that he was so dark.

His darkness was a reminder he was not truly alive anymore in my time. My brightness was a reminder I was not alive yet in his.

My happy thoughts faded as I remembered him talking about

how he was living on borrowed time, and maybe he had gone against the natural order and might have a price to pay.

I bent down and pressed my cheek to the side of his. "What was it you needed help with?"

His hands pulled my hips closer to his. "I wish I could talk tae ye about it now, as ye are in a willing mood, but I find myself with a deeper desire."

I kissed his lips and his tongue slid into my mouth as he pulled me closer. His hands massaging over my chest and down my sides, over my hips and thighs until I raised up and sat down on him with a small gasp. I folded down and we rocked against each other. Pushed and pulled. It was sweet and slow, but tears mingled with my sweat and dripped onto his face because he was leaving. Always leaving.

When we were done, he pulled away to try to see my eyes. "You are crying, Kaitlyn?"

I nodded against the stubble on his jaw.

"Can ye tell me?"

"I just promised I wouldn't say anything."

"I dinna ask ye nae tae speak, I asked ye nae tae argue."

I sobbed. "It feels like every moment with you is saying goodbye."

"Tis true," he said quietly.

Our darkened moonlit room was still, our voices quiet under the soaring ceiling. Our bed rumpled from love making and just a little over a week ago had been empty. For eight weeks I had been alone. And would be again.

I sobbed and he held me until I was done.

Then he said, "I think all men have this problem — we must consider each and every day our last. We are all of us saying goodbye and if ye consider our good fortune, Kaitlyn; I am married tae ye in a second life, three centuries in the future. Our future, our goodbyes, mayna be as final as some."

I said, "Yes, that may be true." To wipe my eyes, I squirmed off him for the tissues on the bed stand, left there from all those nights crying myself to sleep while he was gone.

He adjusted up to the pillows and I joined him. And we lay there together, me wrapped on his whole body. He said, "I canna sleep, would ye come tae the office with me?"

CHAPTER 3

*W*e snuck out of our room and crept up the stairs to the upper floor, trying to be quiet, because Zach would —

Zach stuck his head from his door. "Magnus, sir, do you need anything?"

Magnus chuckled, "Chef Zach, you art a good man. I would like a beer brought tae the office. Kaitlyn?"

"I'd like one too Zach, thank you."

"No problem, Emma and I are just watching TV."

Once I asked Zach why he jumped up to ask if we needed anything, day or night, and he told me it was the least he could do. "Magnus pays me really well, I mean, you and Magnus pay me really well. And Emma. And we live here — we have no bills. And all I have to do is cook meals. That's it. I figure if Magnus needs something in the middle of the night that's easy enough."

In the office Magnus sat behind the desk, I pulled up a chair beside and put my feet in his lap. A moment later Zach appeared with two beers, a platter of cheese, and a small pile of cookies. Magnus laughed. "You know my tastes."

I laughed too. "And mine, the chocolate cookies are definitely for me. What are you and Emma watching?"

"She's making me watch the Crown. We watched the Walking Dead, and now we have to watch what she wants to watch." Zach said to Magnus, "It's about Queen Elizabeth. The *second*." He chuckled as he left the room.

Magnus watched him go. "Tis an odd thing for Chef Zach tae say. You dinna think he knows do ye?"

"I've noticed he makes some odd jokes like that, and he is very high right now."

"High?"

"Yes, he's been smoking pot. Or wait, probably eating it. I don't know, and I've never asked to join in. They do it at night, off work, of course."

"What is it, you haena explained fully."

"It's marijuana, a drug that makes you giddy and floaty, a little like alcohol."

"Ah, but merry-wina dinna explain whether he knows I have journeyed through time."

"I'll call him back in. This will be fun."

I crossed the room and stuck my head into the hall. "Zach, can you come in here?"

Zach entered a moment later. His eyes were bloodshot, and he hid a giggle between his pursed lips.

"Zach, what year is it?"

"2017."

"What year is it for Magnus?"

He looked at me warily. "I don't know, um 2017?" He clamped his lips between his teeth.

"You can speak freely. Magnus knows what year he was born in. I know what year he was born in. Maybe you would like to make a guess?"

"Like 1774 or something. I don't get it, but like from a long,

long, long fucking time ago — he's old as the hills. Oops, sorry sir, Magnus sir, you're young of course, like twenty-three, but you seem to be from a long time ago, probably. I mean if those things weren't improbably impossible."

Magnus met my eyes. "I am older than that. I was born in the year sixteen eighty one."

Zach said, "Whoa seriously? I'm right? Are you shitting me? Like really?" He grabbed a chair, pulled it to the desk, and leaned in. "How? Are you guys fooling me?" He looked to each of our faces.

I shook my head. Magnus shook his too.

"Emma is going to be so pissed. I told her, and she told me I was crazy. But I knew it."

I asked, "When did you figure it out?"

"One night Emma and I had just gotten this job, and we were up talking, and it came to me. Since then I've just believed it more and more. Whoa, that is so cool."

"We can't explain it right now. We have things we're talking about, and we need you to keep this just between you and Emma and us. Even if other people guess, I need you to deny it, okay? But I think it is helpful that you know because you can help deflect questions."

"Sure, of course. I would love to know though, is it like a witchcraft kind of Harry Potter magic, or like Star Trek kind of space and time jumping?"

"Let's go with Star Trek. Right, Magnus?"

Magnus shrugged. "I haena any idea what ye are talking of."

Zach said, "See? Anybody can figure it out." He started to leave.

I asked, "Hey Zach, do you have any extra pot, maybe Magnus can try a bit?"

His eyes went wide. "Um, to be honest, I don't know what the correct answer is."

"You're not in trouble, Magnus's just never tried it, and I thought he might like to."

Magnus asked, "He could buy some for me at the store?"

"No, it's illegal."

Zach shifted his feet. "Promise I'm not in trouble?"

"I promise."

He disappeared down the hall and brought back a small brownie. "You may want to split this, it's potent."

"Thanks Zach, that's all."

After Zach left the room, Magnus said, "Why would a cookie be illegal?"

"I'm not sure how to explain that without some kind of history of the world and since it will need to include Harry Potter and Star Trek too, we might better save it for another day. Pot is becoming legal in many places. California for instance." He leaned forward to break off some brownie. "Wait on that Magnus, until we discuss what you need my help for."

"Och aye." Magnus took a swig of beer and turned to the safe. "I need your help with understanding the vessel."

He twisted the safe's lock back and forth and opened the door. Inside was a small fabric bundle. He gingerly placed it on the desk, untied the fabric, unwrapped it, and spread it open. In the middle was the small tube he had been carrying when he time-jumped a few days earlier. It was metal. In size it was a lot like a Red Bull energy drink can, no logo, very shiny, perfectly formed. The ends had no lip, no seams. It stayed stationary and didn't roll.

"This is it? Does it open or anything?"

"Aye. I twist it in the middle and lights shine forth. Then the vessel warms up and tis as if it melts. The shape transforms into a fit for your hand. Much like quicksilver. Then it rips ye from your own time."

I poked it.

"Pray daena touch, Kaitlyn."

"But touching it doesn't make you time jump, right?"

"Nae, ye have tae recite many numbers as well. But I daena touch it to be safe."

"Okay, but what numbers?"

"I have already taught ye some of them when I taught ye tae use the safe."

"So they're the same, it's like a combination lock."

"And then I come forward or go back in time. But always tae the same location and there is my problem. I arrive on the grounds of Castle Talsworth, the home of Lord Delapointe. And the journey is terribly painful. When I returned tae my time, in the middle of the castle grounds, I was captured easily. I couldna mount a defense I was so weak. The men that came forward through time the day after our wedding were so weak I fought them easily—"

"That was easy?"

"Aye," he said solemnly. "I am trying tae figure how tae journey to a different place. I could rest until I am able tae fight. I would much like tae arrive at Balloch. I could convince Uncle Baldie and my cousins tae help me mount an attack. But I daena understand where the controls are, how tae alter the vessel's course."

I poked the box again. It rolled, a tiny bit, but righted itself, or pulled short. Despite Magnus's groan I picked it up and placed it in the palm of my hand.

"Where did it come from?"

"My father gave them tae my mother when I was a wee bairn."

"Where is he now? He could probably explain it to you—"

"He is deceased."

I squinted my eyes. "Really?"

"Lady Mairead told me he is."

"Hmmmmm. The problem with that is she's not to be trusted. He's likely a time traveler, what if he returned to the future-future?"

Magnus stared at me.

"It makes sense right? If he traveled back in time to bring you the vessels and died there, the whole thing would be screwy. I think he may have returned to the future."

"My father may be alive?"

"Well, not yet. But in the time where they make tech like this. Someday."

"They daena have tech such as this here?"

I smiled. "No, this is way advanced. Way past an iPhone. Time travel is impossible. As a matter of fact it's so impossible that no one will ever believe you. Except Zach of course."

"And ye."

"I married you before I found out. Now it's the only thing that makes sense, but if someone had told me this when I first met you I would never have believed it. Time travel is completely impossible."

"Thank ye for believing me."

"Well, it's the only explanation for the fact that you have never seen a television before."

He smiled. "I knew there was much I dinna figure, but..."

The vessel was solid metal, but also had a bit of vibration. Like it was alive, filled with a hum. It felt like it was on the edge of changing to something else. And the interior moved, or spun. I just couldn't feel it with my senses. Almost like I felt it inside my body instead of on my palm.

He said, "Maybe if I took a horse through with me, as those men did. I might be better able tae fight."

I nodded. "You could, but still, the whole fighting-as-soon-as-you-get-there thing has me really... You say it's very painful?"

"As if your soul has been ripped from the body and then stitched back in." His brow drew down as he said it.

I gulped. "So you could take a horse. But more importantly it would be good to program this vessel to a different landing place. What if the numbers could be changed, perhaps that would— Let's see there's a three—"

"Kaitlyn! Daena say them!"

"Okay, yeah, sorry." I rolled the vessel gently to the fabric on the desk. "Ummm, and Lady Mairead never told you that there were more numbers, a different order, anything else?"

"She only gave me these. Though she is nae tae be—"

"Trusted. Yeah, exactly."

We sat for a few moments. "Maybe you have to jump from a different place here to get back there. We could drive west, plot it on a map; you could jump from Tallahassee or something. The only way to know for sure is to test it, scientifically."

"I would prefer nae tae land in the ocean. I am nae a strong swimmer."

"Oh god, I didn't even think of that. Yes, no landing in the ocean. Can you show me where in Scotland the castle is where you appear?" I pulled the laptop to my knees and opened a map of Scotland. Magnus described where the castle would be. I found the general area, then looked on Wikipedia and found the closest town. The town's main page listed the ruined castle as an 'interesting historic walk.' I hit the plus sign four or five times until I came to a satellite image of overgrown fields around a low ruined stone wall. I took a deep breath and turned the laptop toward Magnus.

"'Tis a ruin."

"Yep."

"The castle that has caused so much of my misery. Where I have been beaten and imprisoned that houses my enemy — tis a ruin. I should feel good, but all my life is a ruin. Maybe I am even buried there under the years of earth."

"Magnus, don't talk like that. I can't bear it."

"I think, when I am gone this time, ye should look for my name in the histories. Find out how I have died. It might answer your questions, mo reul-iuil."

"I won't. You're alive. If you're in Scotland in 1702, or here, you're alive in both places, at the same time. I won't talk about your death. I won't."

I jotted down the latitude and longitude of the castle and the latitude and longitude of Amelia Island, hoping to make some sort of sense of the numbers, but only one number was similar. I couldn't trust a pattern. "Where would you like to go, if my terribly uneducated plan works?"

"To Balloch Castle, my uncle will help me gather men."

I googled the name and found a new building, Taymouth Castle, had been built on top of the old. It was gorgeous. The wealth was astonishing, all these years later. It made me feel a little better that some of Magnus's past didn't end in defeat. "How many castles like this are there?"

"Too many tae count. My family, our family, is verra powerful. It has angered my cousins greatly that they canna keep my mother safe. But she haena told them of the secrets she is keeping."

I plotted the points of Balloch castle and Amelia Island and using my calculator came up with numbers that I jotted down on scrap paper. I checked my numbers three times. "I feel like someone with some knowledge of cartography should double check this before we rely on it, but I think I know where we could try. This little town outside of the Osceola National Forest, here." I pointed at the screen.

"I could ride there by horse and then—"

I shook my head. "We'll take the horse by trailer. It will take an hour or so. I'll drive. We'll kiss goodbye like civilized people, and then you'll go. I'll load your pockets with all the guns you can carry." On my list, below the numbers, the name of the town, "rent a horse trailer," and "kiss goodbye," I wrote "guns" and circled it twice.

"Nae, I canna carry guns. Tis too dangerous. I am trying tae keep your weapons away from the past."

"Oh. Yeah, I guess that makes sense." I drew an angry deep line through the word. "But we still kiss goodbye."

"Aye, because our marriage is nae horseshit."

"True." I leaned back in the chair. He bundled up the vessel, carefully replaced it in the middle of our safe, and closed the door with a slam. He leaned back in his chair. I put my feet on his pajama clad thighs. Plaid, because I thought it was funny when I asked Emma to order them. "When will you go?"

"Soon mo reul-iuil, verra soon."

"On that note." I reached for the brownie, split it down the middle, and passed him half. We ate and then swigged from our beers.

He said, "Shall I order more beer?"

"Let's head down to our room, we can grab our own when we pass the fridge."

"Chef Zach will be outraged if I do things for myself."

We clamored down the stairs with Zach calling behind us, "Need anything, Magnus, sir?"

Magnus chuckled. "Nae, Kaitlyn and I are just taking beers for our room, thank ye." We grabbed two more beers and tucked into our bed.

CHAPTER 4

$\mathcal{W}$e had never really watched TV together because what would Magnus find interesting? Definitely not the Walking Dead. Probably not even Friends. Or the Office. He would have no context. I wondered about trying old school like The Lucy Show, but thought the vintage aspects might be confusing. So I chose SpongeBob. I figured it was silly, and there wasn't an intricate storyline to follow.

I leaned back on the pillows and Magnus laid his head on a pillow on my lap, curled on his side. "Explain it tae me then?"

"He's a sponge under the ocean, and that's his friend, the starfish, Patrick."

"Such as the ones on the wall downstairs?"

"Just like that, except this one talks. And that's Squidward. He hates them and — just watch, try to enjoy the silliness of it. Oh and SpongeBob works at a hamburger restaurant. You'll see." First joke and I was giggling much more than the joke called for.

By the third joke Magnus was laughing too. At one point I paused the show to giggle. "You came forward in time three hundred years, and the best of culture I'm showing you is

SpongeBob!" I laughed so hard I started to cry. It was a relief to be happy-crying instead of sad.

Magnus turned his back to the TV and watched me laugh.

He laughed at me while I laughed at the show, and then I laughed at him while he laughed at me. "You art funnier than the show."

"Really?" I snorted and beer dripped from my nose. Then I giggled more.

Magnus laughed at me more, and we sat together laughing at each other for a long, long time.

Finally I ended with "phew!" and we quieted. "I'm super stoned."

He said, "If that is what tis called, then me as well." He raised the beer to his lips and drank.

"Promise me you won't leave me when I'm high like this."

"I promise. But you canna stay high tae keep me here."

"I promise." I turned SpongeBob back on. "Just tonight, so we can think about something else."

"Och aye, tis good." He leaned forward and kissed me, his lips wet with beer and warm breath and sexy uncontrollable desire. He rose, pulled me by the ankles down flat on the bed, and climbed on my body. We kissed for a long time. It was so sensual, kissing him tasting and licking. It all felt good and new and slow and patient and lasted for a long, long luxurious time. The SpongeBob episode ended, and a new one started. Magnus climbed down my body to kiss my belly. Then he blew into my skin making a fart sound, and we both giggled hysterically. He held me around my hips, his stubbled cheek nestled in the soft area of skin on my pelvis. I giggled, my hand on the back of his head.

He looked up at me and smiled, then lowered farther down and blew, making another silly noise between my legs. I giggled a lot. He said, "You make sounds like the sponge."

I caught my breath. "You're so romantic."

Then he kissed me there, for the first time. My back arched, my head grew dizzy.

"Och aye, I dinna know this."

I managed to gasp, "What?"

"That tae kiss ye here makes ye wiggle and squirm ev'n more." He nuzzled into me. "Was a secret I am just now learning."

I gasped, "No secrets," and then I careened away, lost in the moment, in him, in our room. And after he finished with me, I introduced him to his own secrets, in turn, giggling and silly, and then serious, and oh so feeling good, SpongeBob flickering quietly in the background.

CHAPTER 5

I woke with an idea. "Magnus?"

He grumbled awake, smacking his lips, face pressed into the pillow. He was sleeping on his front to protect his wounded back. He immediately slid closer and put an arm across my stomach.

"Magnus, I have an idea."

"Umhmmm."

"Magnus, what if I went with you—"

His eyes opened, focused, sharp.

"Hear me out — I could help. If you found the vessels, or clues, or needed to figure something out — I could help. Plus I can train. Quentin is buying swords and knives for you today. We could start training me, and then I could —"

He raised up over me to a sitting position. "No Kaitlyn. You canna come. You daena know what ye are saying, tis dangerous. Verra dangerous. Ye canna."

"But by yourself it's more dangerous, with the two of us—"

"I daena know if ye can journey tae my time. What if tis impossible? What if ye are lost forever?"

"I don't think — I think I could..."

"I canna risk it. I have come forward, but dinna ken if ye can go back. I winna risk your life. And if—"

"Your father gave those boxes to your mother. I established last night that *he* went back in time."

He pushed his hand through his hair. "You dinna ken how he accomplished this magic. He may have done the work differently. I canna risk it. And when ye are back in my time — you daena understand how different it is there. I would have tae protect ye. You would be as a child."

"It would be better than waiting."

"It winna be better. I can think of a hundred ways ye could die, just sitting here, and I haena gotten started with the thinking of it."

But you don't have to sit here waiting — not knowing if someone I love is dead or alive."

"Och aye, you are right. But I have tae leave ye. Tis many times harder."

"But—"

"Please, Kaitlyn, I canna argue with ye about it, please."

Those blasted tears welled up again. My throat grew tight. It had all seemed so sensible when I was lying there, waking up, but now... "Okay, fine."

He tried to make it up to me by saying the stupidest thing ever. "Would you want a party?"

I cut my eyes at him. "No, not, I'm not in a party mood *at all.*"

"Och aye." He put his elbows on his knees. "I thought perhaps a party might be a good idea. I am only just here for a short time and—"

"Oh, I thought you were suggesting it for me."

"I would like tae see ye happy, mo reul-iuil. And I would like tae do something besides worry. Being home again feels like a thing tae celebrate."

I climbed up and held on around his shoulders, mindful of his back. "Of course, let's throw a party."

He patted the back of my arm. "Thank ye."

"You're welcome. And I'm sorry about the rollercoaster of emotions I'm on. It's hard to talk about you leaving when you're only just now home and..."

"I feel much the same way, the exception being I haena idea what that is."

"Rollercoaster?"

He nodded.

"Oh man, that's going on the list of things I need to introduce you to. Imagine this — a manmade contraption, steep hills and valleys, and a small cart that shoots around it on a track."

"And people go inside this cart?"

"Oh do they, they pay top dollar to strap themselves inside and go at high speeds, sometimes they are upside down."

"I believe you are making this up."

"I'm not, it's fun. Really, really, really fun. I'll take you someday."

One of his bandages had peeled up. I pulled a corner and checked the wound under it. It looked better, less oozy, though it wasn't one of the deepest. Those were through the middle. This mark crossed his shoulder, and I could already tell it would leave a nasty scar. Thick and raised.

"When you return. When you've secured all the horcruxes, or whatever, and your life is less exciting. We can look for our thrills elsewhere; I'll take you to Disney World and Universal studios. Maybe Cape Canaveral too. Want to see rocket ships?" I opened the box of bandages and tape that sat on the nightstand.

"Rockets tae go up into the air? You arna planning tae strap me inside one?"

"God no, but yes, to a rollercoaster. I'm going to strap you into one."

"You will be right next tae me?"

"Yep, listening to ya scream like a baby."

I patted the bandage down and kissed his shoulder. "Perfect."

"I was also thinking I would like some new clothes."

I climbed off the bed and stood in front of him hands on my hips. "New kilts? Emma had to get those special ordered. They wouldn't be here by the party."

"Nae, new clothes such as Master Cook wears or Master Peters."

"Yes! Oh yes! But not like James; he wears pink golf shirts. Okay, awesome, new clothes and a party!" I spun out of the room for the bathroom and raced back. "Want to join me?"

"You ken the answer is aye, but with my bandages my showers need tae be more careful."

"I'll keep it running for you when I'm done."

CHAPTER 6

Quentin came to work that morning with a new sword and dirk for Magnus. To celebrate, after breakfast, Magnus practiced sparring with Quentin and the other guard. Then Magnus ran all of us through some exercises and sparred with us each in turns. I was still a beginner and that sucked. In my imagination I was a necessary part of Magnus's return to the past because of my swashbuckling skills. I assumed my abilities included jumping over furniture while swinging my blade in a cutting arc because I watched a lot of superhero movies. That had to count for something. Instead my arms were jelly within a few minutes even with the lighter practice swords. Zach easily knocked the blade from my hand. I glanced at Magnus. He looked away and called the practice over.

Emma and I were measuring Magnus and googling men's sizes because all his clothing purchases up until now had been for kilts and had been easy — how long from your hip to your knee?

I used a measuring tape and called out numbers to Emma. She in turn called out the sizes as I jotted them on a list.

When I measured his inseam, Magnus joked, "Make it short, there needs tae be some movement there."

I joked back, "There won't be any movement once we get you in a pair of tighty-whities."

"I daena like the sound of that, tighty?"

"Form-fitting. All the men wear them."

Zach said, "Not me, I'm a boxer shorts guy."

Magnus pointed at Zach. "Och aye, Chef Zach is a man. You daena like the tighty undergarmies?"

Zach laughed. "Nope, I agree on the movement, especially when you work all day in a hot kitchen."

"See?" Magnus wiggled his hand toward me. "I am a boxer shorts man, add tae my list."

"Okay, your waist is a thirty-three. Your chest is um—" I wrapped the tape around his chest and called out, "Forty-eight inches."

Emma fanned herself. "Jesus Christ, really?"

Zach laughed. "You know you prefer men like me. I'm thirty-one inches around at every point on my body, like a flag pole."

"You are much the dimensions of a flagpole, how tall are ye?" Magnus asked.

"Six foot six."

"You aren't much shorter." I pushed Magnus to a wall and made Zach mark with a pencil just over Magnus's head. Then he and I measured from the ground to the mark. "Six foot three and a half."

Then we went to Target for boxer shorts and socks and then the local surf shop.

I picked out a pile of pants in his size plus four shirts and piled them on his arm. "What's this then?"

"You'll go in the tiny room there and try it all on."

"You will come with me? I daena know the way."

I sighed more because of how cute it was than out of irritation. The dressing room was very, very small. It had a curtain that barely closed, and Magnus could see the shop over the top of the curtain rod. "This is going to be hard," I said, as I pulled the bottom of his linen shirt up off his head and arms. It was a struggle to keep it from scraping his bandages.

But then because his awesome chest was right there in front of me, I brought my hands down his sides rubbing down his abs to the front of his kilt. I shoved it to the ground.

"Aye, it will be if ye rub me like that."

I giggled.

"I meant, hard getting you dressed in such a small room, but yes, I see." I giggled again.

"I daena know what is funny — ye have me naked." He chuckled. "Tis usually a promise."

I put a finger to my lips. "Shhh. They'll hear you. And you're not really supposed to be naked, you're supposed to have underpants on."

He pulled my hips close to his front as I pulled a shirt off the hanger. I tugged the shirt over his head, and down over his chest with a couple of quick movements. It was good I removed his skin from such close proximity because I was one centimeter away from pressing my lips to his chest. After that there would be no way to stop me.

I ripped open the bag of boxers we purchased and held a pair low so he could step into it. He jokingly brushed his dick against my shoulder, and I stifled a laugh. "Oh my god, Magnus, you're going to get us in trouble."

He looked around the shop. "What — that I am trying tae get dressing in a wee room and I am bumping my wife?" He bumped me again. We both laughed. "This room is too wee for my—"

"Shh. You're incorrigible." I pulled the boxers up and

snapped the elastic on his waist. "There, you're clothed, you can behave like a civilized Highlander."

He grinned.

I got him into an outfit and it was perfect — a pair of jeans and a shirt with buttons and a collar. They were super sexy on him. I wouldn't have believed covering Magnus up more would improve him, but there was something really awesome about the way the jeans moved on his body.

Except when he stepped out of the dressing room to show me; he pulled at the crotch and kicked a leg to the side. "Tis how it must be worn?"

"Yes. Here, wiggle your hips, let yourself fall one way or the other." He performed a silly hip wiggle.

The proprietor of the shop, an older woman I had known for years, laughed. "Has he never worn pants before?"

"There's a first time for everything."

He wiggled again. "Perchance I need tae put the kilt back on til the party."

I shook my head, "I seriously think you need the practice."

"Now I know why the men here are so serious. They have tae think about what is happenin' with their whirlies."

I rolled my eyes laughing and we went to the counter with what we were going to buy. Jenny introduced herself to Magnus and while he went to look at a display of baseball hats, she said to me in a whisper, "I heard about the kidnapping."

"Yes, we're really glad to have him home."

"I can imagine, that must have been terrifying."

"It was, but now he's back, we're. . . " My voice trailed off. What were we doing, planning his next departure? Yeah, that's what we were doing.

Jenny asked, "Will you both be at the concert next weekend?" She gestured at a flier for one of the local bands.

"Nah, I don't think Magnus will be here. He works a lot out of town."

"That must suck." She tallied our total on the cash register, and I handed her my card.

"He has business in Scotland, it takes him back there a lot," I said again.

She repeated, "Oh man, I would hate that. I like having my man here where I can keep an eye on him."

I nodded and signed the receipt.

When we got in the car, Magnus asked, "Those are questions ye are often asked, mo reul-iuil? Tis how ye often answer?"

I nodded as I started the car. "Everyone heard about your kidnapping, so they ask, sure. Plus, now I have to tell all of Fernandina that your work keeps you out of town. I'll need to lie and pretend that I talk to you. It's just —" I pulled the car onto Fletcher Drive. "It's a really small town, people talk. I have to make sure the talking doesn't — you know, let's not talk about it anymore. Let's talk about how you just bought clothes that I want to immediately rip off your body."

"Aye." He smiled sadly, just before he closed his eyes for the ride home.

CHAPTER 7

$\mathcal{W}$ e were ready for the party and the guests began to arrive. I loved being a hostess, and especially this way, rich as all get out. I was able to make a sweeping gesture toward the kitchen — "If you need anything Zach will help you." Toward the deck — "If you'd like a drink, Emma will serve you."

At first everyone was awkward with Magnus. The last they had seen him was in the hospital delirious. They had visited to say, "Hey man, glad you made it back." And then they hugged me, talked to me, commiserated with me, comforted me. As they had been doing for so many long weeks.

Because the last time they really saw Magnus he was fighting a life and death battle right in the middle of downtown. Then he disappeared. No one was quite sure of the correct words for, "What the fuck just happened?"

And I had already told them what happened. He was a very rich royal, he had been kidnapped and held for ransom. Apparently it was very common this kind of thing, which is why he always had heightened security. His family paid the ransom and then he had been dumped on the beach.

Quentin nodded along. This kind of thing happened all the time in world politics. James seemed skeptical, but what else would explain it? And Hayley had accepted it as, of course, that makes perfect sense.

Magnus talked, he joked, he asked questions about James's work, about Michael's job, and especially focused on Hayley, complimented her, teased her. Within an hour he was a friend again, and everyone appreciated having him back. Especially in the new clothes.

Because as Hayley put it, "That man is heart-stoppable hot. Seriously, Kaitlyn, you gotta put a leash on him and make him stay."

"I kind of have, what with the whole marriage thing. But also, staying isn't really an option right now."

"What do you mean?"

"He has business in Scotland. He has to go back, probably this week, and it may take a while."

"But you just got him back! Magnus, are you leaving us?" Hayley pouted petulantly.

"Och aye, I have business in Scotland. I must return."

James joked, "Married life too boring, you rushing back to the highlands to get away?"

Magnus held my hand tightly. "I daena want tae leave her, but I must."

Hayley turned to me. "You aren't going to go with him, see Scotland? I bet it's beautiful."

"No, I have work, running the estate, keeping the house. I have to keep Zach in work, so yeah — hey, Magnus, do you need another beer?"

I escaped to the house. Emma poured beers into glasses. "He's really leaving again?"

"In a couple of days."

"I'm sorry, it's been nice to have him home. And we'll keep working, right?"

"Yep, at the thought of losing Zach as his private chef, Magnus wanted to sign him right there for a ten year contract. You both have a job, a home, no worries."

"How long will he be gone?"

"Could be weeks or longer. I don't know, he has something big that needs to be handled with his family business."

"Oh," she gestured she would carry the beers out for me. "I guess we need to start thinking of you as the boss instead of Magnus; we've worked for you longer. He just seems like he's the guy we work for."

I chuckled, "True, I'm a bit boring to cook for; he has enthusiasm. It makes us all want to do things for him."

Buffalo wings were passed around, walks on the beach were had. The night started with forty people but dwindled past eleven o'clock to about ten people. The core group with a couple of stragglers. A game of Cards Against Humanity was played. Magnus remained a spectator because, as he put it, "I canna make sense of it. Tis scandalous." Then James got a hold of the speakers and connected his Spotify playlist to them and turned on a song that was deep, deep country.

Magnus sang along.

I dropped my cards and opened my mouth in feigned outrage. "How do you — what?"

Magnus sang a few more lines. "Master Cook played it for me, tis a verra good song. It played in my head over and over while I was away." He sang, ". . . driving in my pickup truck."

I said, "Zach, do you hear this? All your music history lessons for nothing — Magnus likes country."

Zach shook his head sadly as he spooned ice cream into bowls. "Magnus, sir, I played you Nirvana, the Beatles, you prefer pickup trucks, *really*?"

"Listen, Chef Zach. He has a truck and also a beer. The woman he loves has gone away, tis verra poetic."

We all burst into laughter.

James said, "You sound like Shakespeare most of the time, and you think *this* song is poetic? Well, you might be a little delusional, but your taste is headed the right direction." He held up a beer toward Magnus. "To the Scottish farm boy-king and his love for American country music."

We all laughed more and for a while, with the game, and the music, and the beer, we were laughing a lot. For much of the night I completely forgot to be depressed.

Michael said, "Kaitlyn and Magnus, Hayley and I were hoping to have Zach and Emma to dinner tomorrow night?"

Magnus said, "I believe tis my last night."

"Zach does deserve a day off though, and I've never cooked for you. Some people say I'm pretty good. I mean, I'm no Chef Zach, but I could make you something special for your last night."

Emma said, "If you'll give me a list I'll pick up the food for you."

"Awesome, I'm really good at chicken breasts, but buy lots of ice cream just in case the chicken is lame."

Magnus kissed my fingertips. "I would like that."

CHAPTER 8

$\mathcal{T}$he next evening we had the house to ourselves except for Quentin stationed on the back deck. I cooked. Magnus perched on a barstool watching, and then we ate at the kitchen island because it was reminiscent of that night we became friends, so many weeks ago. It also wasn't that long ago, really. We talked about how quick it had been — we met and then in a month we were married. Two months passed while we were apart and now this time, less than a week.

The end of June to the beginning of September, barely any time at all. But also three hundred years.

Still, we had been in the same house, under the same roof, while married, for just a little over a week.

We were still just getting to know each other.

When I said that to Magnus he said, "While that may be the truth of it, I find I canna imagine living without ye, Kaitlyn. When I was imprisoned at Talsworth I kept it in my thoughts that ye were nae yet born, and that ye were safe and would grow up in a future where ye winna need me. But I am selfish and wanted to come back because ye are everything tae me."

My eyes misted. "You were thinking about me while you were singing your favorite song about your pickup truck?"

"Aye, because ye must drive it." He smiled at me, a smile full of love and sadness and longing so I climbed onto his lap and kissed him. Deep and passionate. His hands tucked around my butt and pulled me closer, settling me down. I whispered into his ear. "Are you done with dinner?"

He nodded, his unshaven jaw rubbing along my cheek, his breath warm on my skin. "I am, twas delicious."

I pushed his plate, his beer, and his utensils away across the counter. Then I didn't put my feet down on the ground, instead I stood balancing on the rungs of his barstool and climbed across to the counter. And sat. I spread my legs and leaned back on my hands.

He stood and folded onto my body. "You are full of surprising moments, Madame Campbell."

He kissed down my neck to my shoulder, pressing and pressing, and—

"Are you talking about my deft game of Lava Tag, just now?"

There was a long pause where he kissed and nibbled along my shoulder and neck, and oh god I wanted him so badly.

He mumbled, "What is this — Lava Tag?"

I arched back. "A childhood game where kids pretend like the ground is covered in lava. They can't touch it, so instead they climb everywhere, you know," I gasped as he sucked on the edge of my neck, "seriously unimportant. A minute ago I felt like joking, now I ..." He pressed against me again, and I moaned.

He raised my shirt just a bit and kissed my cleavage along the top edge of my bra. I arched to meet his lips. He spoke into my flesh, his breath hot on my chest. "I was speaking about the surprise of finding your legs spread wide upon my dinner table." His arms tightened around my back pulling me close to his mouth, him. The scent of our dinner lingered in the air around us, the dim light of our kitchen, and the soft hum of the refrigerator set the mood. A candle flickered nearby. Also nearby, his security guard.

I whispered, "Quentin is right outside."

His head drooped on my chest as he pulled my shirt down to cover me. "Aye, and my castle walls are made of glass." He pulled away a bit, his desire plain under his kilt. "If you were wearing a skirt, we might accomplish this without excessive nakedness."

"Ah, but Master Campbell, what is the fun in that?"

He groaned. "Do I carry ye tae the bedroom or ask Quentin tae go tae the beach for an hour?"

I leaned forward, kissed his jawline and down his neck, loosening his shirt and rubbing my hands up under it to the small of his back, pulling him toward me again. I whispered, "I'll wait for you right here."

He pushed away, blew out a breath of air, ran a hand through his hair, and straightened the front of his shirt. Adjusting it so it covered the front of his kilt. "Aye, daena move."

I said, "Freeze tag," and instantly regretted it, because he paused and looked at me quizzically. "I'll explain later, go go go."

He slid open the door and leaned out. I could hear the indistinct rumble of my husband asking his security guard to disappear for a bit and then the door slid closed and he crossed back to me, waiting, perfectly still on the kitchen counter.

He folded over my body, kissed me deep, and then went primal, shoving my shirt up, unclasping my bra, fondling my breasts, running his hands down my back, cupping my ass, pulling me close, desperate and urgent, and incredibly hot. I held on as he fumbled with my shorts and frantically pulled them down my legs, breathing so heavy and deep and rumbling, and with almost a roar he entered me, my name departing on his breath, "Kaitlyn," he said, and my fingers were wrapped through the back of his hair and I kissed his throat — say it again — Kaitlyn — do you love me?

He pushed and shoved against me pulling me tight toward him, filling me so fully with desire, him, want — I do, I love ye — I arched back, lost in a moan. He kissed my breast as he pushed harder, faster, and more, and collapsed on me as he came to the end with a groan completely spent.

My feet twisted on his back pulling his hips closer, I laid back on the counter, wrapped my fingers through his hair, holding him close, nestled to my chest.

I breathed deeply, warm blood and oxygen flowing through me. Beads of sweat glistening on Magnus's forehead. His skin was warm to my touch, his body, a moment before taut and hard and desperate, and now a moment later soft, relaxed and comfortable. I ran my hands down his arms, massaging his muscles, also tightening my hold.

"I love you too," I whispered.

"I know ye do, mo reul-iuil."

"You do? How do you know?"

He raised his head, his chin nestled on my breastbone. His arms around my back, keeping me arched. "I read it in your eyes. Tis one of the reasons I have loved ye since I met ye." He nestled back into my chest and I kissed the top of his head. Then he pushed away, adjusted his clothing, and picked up my shorts. He slipped them over my ankles and pulled them up while I dropped down into them, pulling my shirt back down.

"If I go put on my pajama pants, can we go for a walk on the beach?"

"That would be good, mo reul-iuil."

CHAPTER 9

I changed into some silk pants, a roomy T-shirt, and a sweatshirt, and Magnus and I walked out onto the back deck. The sound of the crashing waves filled the air. Our interior had been so quiet. The breeze was stiff, but the wind wasn't too cold. We walked down the boardwalk with our hair dancing on the wind.

We passed Quentin at the end of the boardwalk and Magnus directed him to remain there, watchful, while we walked. Then we stepped out on our beach.

The waves were big, crashing, the tide coming in. I led Magnus to the edge of the water and we put our feet in, just at the edge. The water was warm, the breeze cooler, and I huddled my shoulders against the breeze. Magnus put his arms around me, warmth and protection.

I looked up at the sky, my hair flinging. "Whoa, look at the stars."

Magnus looked up at the sky. "Och aye, tis sublime. Wondrous. Tis God's work tae create this majesty. I am lucky tae praise him in two different lifetimes."

I nestled into his shoulder. "Shall we walk or sit?"

"Let's walk for a bit." With his arm around my shoulders, we walked.

I used to do this with friends and boyfriends when I was younger. Now with my husband; walking on the beach in the dark. It had a wonderful quality, nighttime beach walks. I could do it for hours. Best part, there was no chance of becoming lost. A few times I walked past my sand dune, but mostly, once I memorized the shape of the roofline of my house, darker against the moonlit sky, I could find it again. "Tell me three things I don't know about you."

He looked down at me. Then back at the far horizon. "I have a sister and a brother."

"You do?"

"I do. They are older than me. Their father, Lady Mairead's first husband, died when they were verra young. They took care of me when I was a wee bairn before I was sent tae London tae live. When I returned to the Highlands, a few years ago, I spent most of the time with them. My sister, Lizabeth, is kind and funny. She has a baby and a terrible husband. My brother, Sean, is a troublemaker and a ruffian. Do ye know that word?"

"I do."

"He likes to create mischief and fight daily if he can. Tis verra useful tae have him around if ye daena want tae fight. He will take it on for ye." He smiled. "He is good protection for Lizabeth, except was hard for her tae make a match with Sean acting as her guardian."

"This is why you said you could understand a man like James, because you have Sean?"

"And all the other men of my clan. Tis a place full of hotheaded fools and the best of men. Ofttimes within the same body. James would fit in well. Perhaps better than well, he is stupid in the ways of love, but in business I hear he is quite wise. That means something in any time."

"I suppose it does." I kissed the end of his fingers, where they rested on my shoulder. "Tell me two more things."

"I had a girl, in London."

"What?"

"I liked her a bit. I would have married her had someone made me."

"Oh, I never asked, that's..."

"This would have all been different, but instead I was called back to the Highlands, and I left her without a thought."

"Really? That's so callous, so you're kind of a bad boy, huh?"

He looked down at my face and laughed. "What if I had married a girl such as that and had then met ye? It would have been a hard thing tae break a vow."

I laughed this time. "I was thinking you would have honored those vows, that I would have been left out."

"Nae, I would have moved heaven and earth tae make it happen with ye."

"Like Henry the eighth, you would have started a new religion?"

"Is that how the story goes then? Interesting..."

"I wonder if you could ask for a three hundred year divorce in court?"

He chuckled. "Would the pope have tae decide it? Tis how it happens in my day."

"Not here, here the courts decide it."

"Tis easy tae divorce here?"

"Yes, the number is as high as fifty percent."

He hugged me tighter, "I owe ye one more bit of information about myself. Let's see... you will like the humor of this one, I think. The first time I met the Royal Highnesses, the King and Queen of England."

"Which ones?"

He turned to me, "Ah, tis King William the third and Queen Mary."

"Ah, I really only know the Elizabeths if pressed."

"Elizabeths? I see there is much I need tae hear of. Tis an unsettling thing tae have a history I daena know." He picked up a stick and threw it end over end into the waves. "Tis distressing that the royal succession I and my family have cared so much about is of little consequence three hundred years on."

"Puts things in perspective, huh?"

"It must. I have often believed, as a Londoner living in the Highlands, and as a Highlander living in London, that I must choose a side. My thought was I would either need tae become an Englishman or take arms against them. Lady Mairead interrupted my decision when she brought me here, and now, the decision seems at times unnecessary."

"You live here now, you have no side in that fight."

He kissed the top of my head, near my hairline. "The fight rages on without me, and here I walk with my wife, far away — tis true. But my family is taking up arms. I am distant, but I have a bond. I canna hide from it. I have always wanted tae be someone my family can depend on. My brother Sean is trusted and proven, but our fathers are different. I have tae prove my worth despite my lineage."

I said, "Still?"

"Still." A wave lapped over our bare feet, rose to our ankles and then higher to our calves, wetting the bottom of my pajama pants. We laughed and scurried a bit up the slope away from the rising tide. "I am sorry you feel so torn, between homes and times and families."

He dropped to the ground and put out his arm for me to curl under. We sat and looked out on the dark sea, under the black night sky. The wind kept the sky clear of clouds and stars were flung from horizon to horizon. It was beautiful.

"I am nae torn so much. There is only ye, Kaitlyn, but I have a duty tae my family as well."

"Oh." I cuddled into his side, an arm on his knee. "So you met the king and queen?"

"I was livin' near London with my uncle and his five children. I was the eldest and if you pressed them, they would describe me much the way I have described Sean. I was always getting the lot in trouble. Except Mary May, a bonny wee bairn, now twelve, I would guess. She could get away with anythin' because of her sweet smile and cheerful laugh, But all the rest followed me on any misdeed and adventure, and then Uncle John would be furious. He always knew the true culprit though. I would receive my whipping and after that the cousins were always quite kind for a bit. Until they forgot tae be cautious, and I led them awry again.

"I was often at court after, but this time was my first audience with the king and queen, twas verra important and we had tae be well dressed. The fussing over our attire was relentless and lasted for weeks."

"Did you wear a kilt?"

"Nae, breeches and a shirt, with a tight coat. I wore a jaunty bow in my hair. Tiny shoes. Ye would have thought me quite pretty and perhaps nae the suitable marrying type." He wordlessly stood and held down a hand to help me up. I wondered how I could ever not marry him. His wide shoulders would have definitely offset the feminine bow. We began the walk home while he continued, "We all went downstairs to the carriages tae drive tae Kensington Palace and was all good when we arrived, except—"

"Except? Uh oh." I wrapped my arm in his elbow.

"Och aye, there were tiny gravel pebbles underfoot. I deftly scooped up a bit and secretly tossed them at my cousins. A pebble hit Henry in the back of the head and he turned cursing to see where it had come from. A pebble hit the ear of Mabel and rolled down into the front of her dress. I hit cousin Theodore next, then Archibald, and lastly I aimed tae lightly pelt little May. It was fun tae see their outage. But then my cousins ganged against me and as my uncle was on the other side of the carriage helping my aunt step out, they grabbed me about both arms and held me still while Henry dumped a fistful of pebbles down the back of my shirt."

He chuckled. "Then there was nothing tae do but enter the palace for our audience with the king and queen. The entire time I was shifting and writhing as pebbles crawled down the inside of my shirt. A few were in the back of my breeches, some down my legs, and as I bowed in front of King William and Queen Mary, three small pebbles rolled from the bottom of my breeches tae the floor."

"Oh my god, were you mortified?"

"I was, but the queen merely laughed. She asked me what other gifts I had brought. I had nae answer, and had been warned nae tae say a word, so instead I went red-faced and my uncle had tae apologize for my state."

"Oh, that must have been awful!"

"The way home my uncle wanted me tae tell him how the pebbles came tae be inside my pants and I refused tae tell him. He did nae trust me much after that, but my cousins would follow me anywhere."

"That's a nice story."

He laughed. "Tis — unless I need my uncle's help someday." We both laughed. "Now ye owe me three things."

"You've already seen my biggest thing to tell."

"Tis the most shameful thing, nae the most important, if ye daena let it be."

"True, okay, how about this — I used to make movies, whole stories. I would create a script, convince a couple of friends to come over, and pull out a box of dress-up clothes. We would act it out, and I would film it. One of the main reasons I adored Hayley. She would be my lead actress and took it all very seriously."

"Much like a play."

"Exactly. I'll show you one someday. They were very silly."

"Okay, two more things."

"I took ballet when I was a little girl."

"The French fancy dancing?"

"Yep," I spun away and performed two mediocre leaps and very sandy pirouette, but I ended in a perfect pose.

Magnus dutifully said, "beautiful."

Then I had to come up with a last thing. I thought for a few moments before I said, "My grandmother has Alzheimer's."

He looked quizzical.

"It's a disease that takes memories away. My grandmother, Barbara, can remember me as a child, my mother as a child, but when I talk to her now, I have to remind her who I am. It's really hard because until about three years ago she was my favorite person in the world to talk to."

"'Tis a tragedy."

We came to our boardwalk. I climbed a step and turned to face him. "It is. She used to be such a sparkling, funny person. And so smart. She and my grandfather were university professors. They were always reading and learning something new. I thought they were the smartest people in the world, and if they gave me advice I followed it, because they were always right. Now she doesn't even know who I am most of the time. It makes me wonder why our brains would do this? It's so unfair to keep some memories, but lose others, to have these terrible gaps." My voice caught in my throat. "What must it be like to suddenly not remember a person, someone you used to love?"

He wrapped his arms around me. "Where does your grand-mother live?"

"In Maine."

"How far away is it?"

"Thousands of miles. I usually fly when I go to see her." I added, "In an airplane," because his brow furrowed familiarly as he tried to work out what I really meant.

"Maybe she is nae meant tae be so far away. Her memories might be fainter than before, but if ye were nearby she winna have tae peer so far back tae remember ye."

"That's a good point. We thought it was better for her to be in her home, but it might be time for her to move..." I leaned on the railing and looked up into Magnus's eyes, his were concerned. "I'm sorry I brought the whole mood down."

"Talk of our family is important. It may as well happen during a walk on the beach than anywhere else. But this story ye have told me is of your grandmother. I still get tae hear one more thing of you."

"I love to cannonball off my grandma's dock in Maine. I was the—"

"Cannonball?"

"Yes, you jump, grab your knees, tuck your whole body like this, and plunge into the lake. I would do it over and over and over again, just taking a moment to eat and then doing it again and again."

"How auld were ye then?"

"Ten."

"Ah, I can see it."

I rolled my eyes. "You've never seen a cannonball jump, an American lake, a dock, a Maine summer, or a ten-year-old American girl in a bathing suit. I seriously don't think you have any idea what you're talking about."

He chuckled. "I am imaginin' my cousin Mary, jumping into Loch Awe in her full gown, and aye, she has now slipped on the ice, fallen through, and frozen tae death. I suppose I might nae have a clear picture."

"We'll go someday, me and you."

"And then I shall see our children jump off the dock."

I cocked my head to the side. "Do you do that on purpose?"

"What?"

"Say things about our future and love and our family as if it's easy for you — to suddenly be married and thinking about forever with me."

"'Tis the easiest thing in the world. Nae for ye?"

"I just spent two months wondering if I'd ever see you again. I'm a moment from saying goodbye. It's hard to get past how sad I know I'll be in a few hours when you're gone."

In answer he put his arms around me and held me tight to his chest until finally after long moments we turned to walk back to our house.

CHAPTER 10

At about two in the morning I heard quiet sounds from the kitchen. I felt on Magnus's side of the bed. It was empty. I pulled on a t-shirt and pajama bottoms and crept into the living room. Magnus was sitting at the kitchen counter while Zach and Emma were washing our dishes and straightening up from our earlier meal. They were telling Magnus about their evening out.

It was a lovely domestic scene, warm and comfortable, and it came to me finally, truly, how hard it must be for Magnus to leave. This was his home now. I could see it in the casual comfortable curve of his wounded back. Wounds that had been inflicted in his past. He was talking to Chef Zach, his second most favorite person in the world. He was hours away from leaving, yet up, sitting in the kitchen, talking a last long goodbye. I joined him at the counter.

Zach greeted me with, "Flavor?"

I chose chocolate chunk with drizzled caramel. My bowl held two enormous scoops. Magnus's bowl held a gigantic banana split. His face was covered in a wide grin. "I have asked Chef

Zach tae surprise me with ice cream and he created this masterpiece."

Zach said, "Hopefully, this will tide you over while you're away."

"I wish it were so, but tis impossible tae tide m'self when I'm surrounded with dry bread and porridges. I'll miss ice cream a great deal."

"When you return, we should make it. I'll get a churn and you can see the magic of it."

Emma said, "Ooh, or one of those balls. You make ice cream by rolling a ball back and forth."

Zach said, "Definitely, when you come home we'll have an ice cream party."

Magnus and I ate our dessert and listened to stories about the Greene family dinner they had just attended. Apparently it was awful, Zach and Michael's parents were putting the pressure on Michael to marry Hayley.

I said, "Real pressure, like in the middle of dinner?"

"Yep, telling him to get real and marry her already."

"Hayley must have been freaking out."

Magnus asked, "But nae ye, Chef Zach? Ye haena married Emma. . ."

Zach said, "Well... about that. You see, we aren't getting married, but she's um, pregnant."

Magnus jumped from his chair. "Congratulations! Twill be a bairn! Tis braw, verra braw." Magnus swept Zach up into a manly hug and then Emma. Then I hugged Zach and Emma and joked that Emma should be eating the ice cream instead of me.

She said, "Ugh, I can't keep anything down right now."

Zach said, "I know this complicates things — we live here rent free, and a baby is — we'll look for an apartment nearby, but we would like to continue to work for you, Magnus, sir."

Magnus scowled. "I canna understand your words Chef Zach, you art a member of my family. Do I nae pay ye enough?"

Zach said, "You pay me plenty. I just—"

Magnus squinted and shook his head. "In the Highlands if a man lives on the land of another, he is as family. I winna force ye tae leave because of a baby. Tis madness tae suggest it."

I put a hand on Magnus's arm to stay him. "What Magnus is saying, I believe, is that you, Emma, and the baby, are all welcome to continue living here. If you want to. If you think you'd rather have your own private home, we will help in any way. Magnus would, of course, like it if you can feed him ice cream in the middle of the night, possibly forever, but you might need to feed a baby in the middle of the night instead. You and Emma can think of this as your home, but talk it over and do what you think is right in the long run. Also, do you have health insurance through the temp agency, and is it good enough? We might need to go ahead and make you a full-time employee. I'll research the smartest way to handle that." I grabbed a pad of paper and started a list, my third of the day.

At the end of our middle of the night snack, Zach and Emma departed for their bed and Magnus and I went to our room. But it was hard to think about sleeping even though it was very late, or early, depending on your perspective. He climbed into bed, held up an arm, and I curled up under it. And we talked.

He began with, "What did ye mean when ye said 'health' tae Zach?"

"Health insurance, it pays the medical bills for the hospital care. It's kind of confusing, but it's the employer's duty to provide it."

"Aye. I would like for Chef Zach and Emma tae have it, whatever they need. Do ye believe they need bigger rooms?"

"Probably, we could give them Lady Mairead's rooms, they're much bigger."

"Aye, and health assurance. We pay them enough?"

"He says we do. I don't think they were able to get married before, and now they can. I think it's good."

"Quentin as well, he is a good man. I would like him tae have health assurances as well."

"Of course."

"There is enough money?"

"I was going to ask you about that. There are paintings, in the office. I think they belonged to Lady Mairead, I was thinking about getting them appraised — do you know where they're from?"

"She journeyed for them. I would assume they are verra valuable. She studied a great deal."

"Okay, I'll locate an art dealer then." I twisted the cloth of his shirt around my index finger. "Magnus?"

"Aye?"

"My phone number is 310-499-2398. Can you repeat it back to me?"

He did.

I made him repeat it four more times. "You know your address here?"

"Aye. But why do ye want me tae know of this?"

"Because wherever you come back to, I want you to be able to find me. If you end up anywhere in the world, ask someone to call me for you."

"What if tis a different time?"

What if it was a different time?

"Do you remember my maiden name?"

He repeated it, "Kaitlyn Sheffield."

I traced a circle around on his chest. Connecting the dots, building a map to find me. "I was born in 1995. I lived with my parents here in Fernandina beach, Florida, until I was 18. Then I moved to Tallahassee Florida and went to college. In 2014 I moved to Los Angeles, California. I lived there until this summer, 2017." I tried to think of what else I could tell him, to solidify it in his mind. It was simply abstract dates and names, no way to reference it for him.

"My parents, Paige and John Sheffield have lived here since 1990. My grandparents, Jack and Barbara Sheffield, live in Orono, Maine. Can you remember all of this?"

"I will."

"Good."

And we lay there — I reminded him of numbers and dates and told him histories of my life and the others close to me. He repeated softly spoken assurances that somehow, journeying through space and time, using a technology he didn't understand — he would find me again.

The guy from the 1700s. The early 1700s. Born in the 1600s, would find me.

Though he couldn't even grasp the tech of a cell phone.

Though FaceTime freaked him out.

He promised me he would. In the softly growing light of a sunrise sky through our wall of windows on his last night in September 2017 — he promised me.

$\mathcal{W}$e woke slowly and made love quietly, spooned together. That lovely kind where you barely wake but caress and cajole and crave and cuddle through it. No acrobats, no heroics, just slow and simple, wrapped around him within his arms sweetly moving against and with. When we finished, he held me tightly for a long time without words just breaths along my neck, his heartbeat against my back.

I didn't need to hear what he couldn't say. It would break my heart to hear it. And it would break him to speak it. I understood it now. How hard it would be, and all I could do was try to help.

When we finally broke the embrace, he rose and sat on the edge of the bed. I checked his back. It looked even better and after applying some new bandages, he left our bed and began to set aside a few things to take with him. He placed a prescription ointment and some antibiotics in his sporran.

I wondered if that had ever in the history of man happened before?

He laid out his clothes, a kilt and shirt, his cloak, a pair of leather shoes. Everything had been mail-ordered from a site

Emma found and matched what he was used to wearing almost perfectly. The kilt was a single color, deep green, because the only tartans the website carried were associated with clans the Campbells had been feuding with Magnus's whole life.

While he laid out his clothes, I sat on the bed, watching and talking.

I said, "I have the photos of the vessel, the numbers written down, I'll try to figure out how to work it. All you have to do is come back here and I'll have answers when you do. Just come back."

"Aye. Kaitlyn, I will come back. You know I mean tae."

"Repeat to me my phone number, my full name, where I lived just before I moved back here. The date I was born."

He repeated it all perfectly, and we went to the kitchen to eat the goodbye breakfast that Zach had made.

CHAPTER 12

$\mathcal{D}$ebbie from Amelia Island Stables arrived just after breakfast to drop off Magnus's horse, the horse trailer, and truck we rented for the day. It would be my first time driving a truck with a horse trailer, and I thought about asking her to do it for us, but Magnus and I needed to do this alone.

It would be difficult enough to explain that the horse and Magnus were gone when I returned.

While Magnus washed up after breakfast, I tore a strip of leather, about a foot long, off the sheath of one of Magnus's practice swords and carved my initial, K. I wrote 310. . . and the rest of my phone number. It looked terrible, not well-crafted at all. I took a sharpie pen and wrote the number better on the inside and then carved a heart at the end of the number. It was a panic move. I was flailing for ideas. I wished I had engraved his ring with it. Or gotten him a tattoo. Or sewn it into the seam of his kilt.

When he emerged from the bathroom, I showed it to him sheepishly. He nodded and I tied it in a knot around his left wrist.

He put an arm around me, pulled me in tight for a hug, and then we looked around the room for anything else he might need.

He was dressed in his gear, cloak over his shoulders, sword on his back, dirk at his hip, sporran at his waist. His leather shoes. His prescription meds. I remembered he should have a photo. Hayley had framed the photo of the two of us, leaning together the night of our wedding surrounded by the feast. I was in my wedding dress; he was in his wedding suit. We hadn't touched beyond the Handfasting of the wedding, but already we glowed. It looked very much like we were in love.

I could easily print another. I pried the back of the frame and peeled the photo from the matte. I folded it small, careful not to crease our faces. He opened the sporran and I stuffed it in. I glimpsed the vessel nestled inside — ready to be used.

He said, "We should go I think."

"Yes, it's a two hour drive." I grabbed my keys and purse and we headed to the driveway.

Debbie walked us around the trailer, the truck, and explained all the odd things that might go wrong, then she left.

Quentin met with Magnus and received his last orders.

Zach and Emma stood on the driveway to say good bye. I climbed into the driver's seat.

Magnus opened the passenger side door, a second away from climbing in — then he turned, looking over his shoulder, past the house, toward the beach.

When I followed his gaze I saw it, storm clouds, rising roiling rolling out over the sand.

I said, "Magnus?"

He continued to watch the sky, body tense, his expression focused. I asked again, "Magnus?"

He glanced at me across the seat, "I may need tae—"

"The horse, you need the horse and the—"

He turned and ran, fast, under the house, sprinting toward the dunes. His cloak rippling behind him. His arm reaching over his shoulder to unsheath his sword.

"Oh my god, oh my god," It took me two tries to work the dumbass door handle, crash it open, and spill out of the truck to the ground.

"Shit, he's going. Quentin, he's going!"

Quentin raced toward the beach after Magnus with me one second behind. Zach and Emma followed at a run as well. All racing toward the beach and the furious looking storm.

By the time I came over the hill Magnus was roaring down the sand dunes toward a man on horseback.

"Magnus!" I ran harder, not understanding why. What in the world would I do once I got there, watch? I couldn't just watch him fight. I needed a gun. Quentin probably had one. Probably.

Magnus had his sword drawn. As he closed on the man and horse, bellowing wildly, he brought the sword around in an arc, meeting steel with steel. A clanging crash, surrounded by arced lightning. Dark skies. Wind whipped sand in our eyes. The sand-blasting pain bringing the fearful tears that demanded to come.

"Magnus! Come back, we should still go this way; don't leave yet! We have a plan!" My words were whipped around my head and wildly away behind me.

The man who had come from the storm was weak. I could see it, disoriented and dazed, but he was also on high, swinging down against Magnus. Magnus was sweeping up. They fought brutally for long moments, spinning in a circle.

Quentin stood on the dune, not drawing his gun. "Quentin? Shoot him!"

He shook his head.

"Shoot him!" I grabbed his arm, deciding to grab his gun away and shoot the man myself. Because then we would have two boxes. We would only need to find one more. We could take our time.

But Quentin struggled against me. "I'm following orders, Katie." He wrenched my arm behind my back to stop me from grasping at his clothes. "I'm following orders. He told me not to draw my weapon. He doesn't want a body here — any questions."

"You know what Quentin? You're an asshole." I turned as Magnus swept the sword, spun, and whacked it against the man's right arm. The fighter dropped his sword. He grasped his injured arm and slumped forward. Magnus had the reins in his hand. The horse bucked and fought and Magnus pulled attempting to control the crazed horse.

He was trying to get his hand into the man's sporran to find the vessel. He had a foot on the stirrup and was trying to heave himself up while the horse spun and bucked — but then the man grabbed Magnus in a chokehold.

Magnus's feet left the ground kicking the air, and that was all I could watch.

I raced toward him. Quentin yanked the back of my shirt, trying to stop me. The wind rushed toward me. It felt like an uphill climb — the world conspiring against me — but he needed help.

I had to help.

And then worse — Magnus thrust his hand into his own sporran — his lips were moving. He was reciting the numbers while holding onto the vessel about to jump time—

just as my hand grabbed his arm to yank it away.

His eyes,

deep,

dark,

enraged,

met mine and it was —

Too late.

The force of it hit me like a concussion grenade. It slammed into me so brutally my head snapped back. Lifting, stretching, shoving. I was yanked. Something held my wrist painfully tight. Air rushed past. I was thrown left and right. Then my body felt like it would be torn in two, pushed and pulled and ripped into pieces.

And then it got really, really fucking bad. Every nerve, every synapse was twisted. All cells pried up, and every. Single. Bit. Of. Skin singed away.

And that part, it lasted for forever. Just pain, gasping breath, endless buffeting, and screams that went on and on and on — knives in my ears.

Make it stop screaming!

— I wished I could pass out. I begged God or the universe or whoever was in charge of what this was to let me die and please bring on the darkness instead of this piercing red riot of pain.

And that was it for a really, really long time.

CHAPTER 13

"*K*aitlyn! Stop screaming!"

Magnus's muffled voice filled my head. It was me making that noise, but I couldn't stop. Because it wasn't really me screaming, it was my body. I had no control. His hand clamped down on my mouth, hard. I breathed in rasps through my nose against the heel of his hand, trying to make sense of what I was seeing: darkness, his shoulder up against my ribs. Was I up or down and cold — jeez, it was cold. I shuddered against his chest.

He was stone cold still, pressing down, forcing me to not breathe, to not move, to not make a sound. His face emerged from the dim and turned into my focus. His eyes glared. His jaw was set, his lips formed a soundless, "Shush."

I had been moaning. I tried to stop, to go still, to be quiet, but my breath wouldn't stop gasping. My heart banged in my chest. My pulse roared in my ears. I tried to be quiet but everything was terrifyingly loud.

And worse, I couldn't get enough air.

And worse again, the pain rolling me under once more.

CHAPTER 14

agnus shoved away.

His hushed voice said from nearby, "How dare ye, Kaitlyn, how dare ye do this?" He stood over me. Dim through the darkness and my foggy, pain-riddled sight. "I have commanded ye, as my wife — ye have made an oath, in front of God, that ye will obey me and this—" His last words were a growl, "Tis unforgivable."

I heaved a breath from my lungs and gasped for another as my body — limp, damaged, possibly unalterably broken, but definitely paralyzed, at the least — flung up the backside of another wave of pain and then crested and crashed and tumbled down the other side with a moan. I wasn't paralyzed, I could freaking feel everything.

His voice continued, "What, would ye do, Kaitlyn, stop me? You have promised me your devotion. How dare ye. What would ye have me do, watch ye die? Twould be my fault. I canna battle with ye a'holdin' my arm! I canna fight with ye sharin' my horse. You want tae die? You will make me watch it, and you will take me with ye." The tops of trees and a black night sky formed his background. His eyes were furious, his face set. His voice so loud it hurt my ears despite my fists clamped over them tight.

I wanted to answer, to argue, to beg, to do or say anything. But all I could do was clench my whole self against another wave of anguish and to squeak out, "It hurts."

His voice came close. "I have been telling ye. Tis verra painful. I am in the midst of it too." He swept the cloak off his shoulders and placed it over me, tucking it in under my knees and around my back. Then he sank to the ground. His back was to me. His arms were around his knees, sword in his hands. "You need tae rest. If ye wake, and I am nae here, I am attempting tae get a horse. I would ask ye tae bide here and remain quiet, but ye nae mind me, so I will save my words. Tis in your best interest though tae remain unfound."

CHAPTER 15

*T*ime passed; minutes or hours or days, I couldn't tell. I woke occasionally, pulled up the edge of the cloak to check. Magnus was sitting like a sentry in front of me, holding his sword, awake. Until finally after a great deal of time and after the waves of pain subsided leaving me weak and ill, I pried the edge of the cloak away, and he was gone. I was on a forest floor, surrounded by cold damp leaves. The sounds of a dark night, animals hooting and rustling, were magnified around me. I found myself somewhere in time and space, but where? It could be America of course — perhaps a seagull grabbed me by a strand of hair and carried me to Minnesota or some other freezing place. But the pain all over my body? It could only be explained by Somewhere Else.

And now I was alone.

And Magnus was pissed.

I tucked my head to my knees in a tight circle and tried to go completely quiet.

Later, I heard a rustling — and then without warning the cloak was pulled away. Magnus appeared in my still foggy vision. Everything was dark and faint, plus nighttime. He put a finger to his lips to silence me, then held out a hand to help me up. I swayed from the sudden change of position and collapsed against his chest.

He led me to the horse. I was freezing and my head was spinning. Vertigo — I thought I might faint. He wordlessly placed my hands on the side of the horse, shoved my face to the fur, and hefted me on his shoulder up and over. I ended slung over the back of the horse completely stuck. Like a sack of something. My short little sundress and tiny panties on view to the whole entire world. Because it had been a warm day in Florida for September and I had wanted the last thing Magnus to see to be my bare legs. And now he was seeing my bare legs in freaking Scotland, where he expressly, undeniably, irrefutably told me not to come.

And it was so cold. Now that I wasn't in pain anymore, I clenched tight shivering. I wanted to move to sitting but if I went off balance I would fall on my head. If I fell back, it would be on top of Magnus, and then he'd have to heave me back up. So like a sack of potatoes, I lay there doing nothing helpful at all.

Magnus retrieved the cloak and deftly climbed behind me. He shoved an arm under my waist lifting and turning me, so I ended astride the horse. Then he wrapped the cloak around me and tucked it in around my legs. He urged the horse forward into a walk.

Magnus remained perfectly quiet. His arms were around me, pressed to me, arms tight, holding. I knew he was cold without his cloak, but there wasn't any way I could survive without it. The horse picked its way along the roots and rock, the uneven terrain, around trees and fallen trunks. We went slowly in the half-light of predawn. Our 'Not Speaking' continued for a really long time until finally he said, "Are ye cold?"

I shivered a bit, but said, "I'm okay, it's cold, but I'll be okay."

"I canna make a fire. We must put a distance between us and Talsworth. We will arrive at Balloch in about six hours." He turned the horse around a tree jutting into our path.

"How did you get the horse?"

"I have beaten a man for it."

I bit my lip to hold back my tears. What had I been thinking? I had wanted Magnus to be able to trust me to do the right thing. But I had screwed it all up. I was so sure I needed to stop him from going, I went with him. Now I was a burden.

As if he could read my thoughts he said, "I canna risk sendin' ye back now. It would attract attention and I daena know if ye can make the trip."

"I don't want to, it hurts."

"I know. But ye canna stay here. Tis nae safe for you."

I nodded sullenly. I had believed he went back and forth because he liked adventure. There was no way he did that for any reason beyond duty.

He asked, "What do ye have inside your bag?"

I recited from memory. "My wallet, my Burt's Bees lip balm, my phone. Oh, and a protein bar."

"We should eat that. I am verra hungry."

I dug out the bar, ripped open the wrapper, and took a bite. I passed him the rest. I was famished, but he generally ate three times as much as me. I got out my lip balm and smeared it on my lips.

I asked, "What happened with the second vessel?"

"We landed outside the castle walls. Twas dark and the horse was wild. The man fell, injured, but guards were comin'. I dinna have time tae get the vessel. I picked ye up over my shoulder and ran tae the forest."

"While you were in this much pain?"

"Aye. When we get ye tae Balloch we shall decide what tae do with ye."

I went silent and for the next few hours we rode in silence.

CHAPTER 16

*B*alloch castle was amazing — old, big, awesome, and daunting. Towers jutted up beside a wide arched gate. The road carried many people all dressed much like Magnus usually. Except they were smartly bundled in layers of cloaks and wraps. There were many wooden carts, piled high with bundles, pulled by horses. A carriage had just entered the gates ahead of us.

"Keep your head down, Kaitlyn. I will ride fast tae get tae the interior before we are noticed." I pulled the cloak over my face. The steady beat of the horse quickened as we hustled through the crowds, clip clopping over the brick road. We passed through a large gateway and turned right just within. We traveled along the interior wall, keeping to the edges of the wide, crowded courtyard until we came to a dark sheltered spot. Magnus slid off, tied our horse to an iron ring, and put out his arms so I could slide into them. He held me tightly around the shoulders as he hustled me through a series of doors into an even darker, colder interior.

We came to the top of steep winding stairs, rough hewn and uneven, with no railing, and he led me down into what must have been the castle's kitchen. The ceilings were very low. At tables at the far end five women bustled around carrying bowls and pots. Nearby a fire blazed in a circular pit. Three small chickens raced by.

Magnus said, "Wait here," and left my side for the far end of the room where the women worked. I kept the cloak over my head and stared at the ground trying to ignore a chicken that was clucking and scratching perilously close. It squawked and scattered as a small terrier rushed over and pawed my shins, sniffing my sneakers. I hurriedly arranged the cloak to drape, so it hid my shoes but the damn dog was drawing attention to my feet. Wait, now two more dogs joined in, sniffing and circling my legs.

Magnus returned a minute later with an older woman who shooed the dogs away.

Magnus said, "I'll need tae go secure us a room. Madame Dougal has said for ye to wait in the wine cellar. You will be undetected."

The older woman said something unrecognizable though it sounded a lot like scolding. She shook her head and spoke fast and loud with guttural noises that were quite frankly frightening. I suspected she was irritated by me. Perhaps my lack of clothes. My inability to speak the language. My sudden intrusion. Magnus led me with a firm hand on my lower back to a room at the opposite wall of the kitchen. Then through that room to an even larger room containing wooden racks stacked with dusty wine bottles and large casks and barrels. The room was darker still, gloomy, and very cold.

"I winna take long Kaitlyn. I will find a room and procure ye dressings. Then I will return for ye. Once you are in proper clothes twill be easier."

"Okay. Come right back though, this is—"

"I know, tis verra hard, bright and loud and—"

"It's not. It's dark and foggy and everyone is faint. Except for my breathing, my heartbeat, I can hear it too loudly. It's really..." I bit my lip. I had come uninvited. I couldn't expect sympathy.

Magnus closed the front of my cloak. Nodded quietly. "I will hurry."

He slipped away leaving me standing in the cold shadows of an ancient castle, somewhere in the world, somewhere lost in time.

CHAPTER 17

A half hour later or so passed. I was watching the progression of a spider that had decided to scale the shelf nearest me, distressingly close. It was working on a web, disinterested in my growing fear. I was so thirsty. The dusty bottles made my parched mouth even drier, and I had no idea how to open one of these bottles. Was I allowed to open one of these bottles? I was by myself, and I didn't know what the rules were. Footsteps sounded on the other end of the room.

"Magnus?"

A man's voice grumbled, "Who's there?"

I turned to the closest shelves, shielding my face, attempting to pretend to be busy looking over the ancient bottles. There were no labels though, nothing to look at really, just bottles on their sides on wooden shelves under a quarter inch of dust.

Two stumbling steps later a hulking, red-faced man came weaving around a shelf and right up to me. He was big. His nose bulbous and red. His eyes angry. He shifted close and said something loudly to the side of my face in what must have been

Gaelic. I went quiet and continued to look down at the closest shelf.

He grabbed my arm, yanked me around to face him, and spoke again loud and angry.

I shook my head, wildly, and tried to draw from his clutch. It was tight on my wrist and clamping tighter.

He spoke again drawing himself up, bearing down on my face, towering over me.

His breath had that toxic-sweet alcoholic smell of a grotesque hangover, and his eyes had that crazed look someone gets when they've had way too much to drink. I shook my head again and looked away.

His open hand swung and clapped me on the side of my head, hard.

I shrieked, clutching my face. The shock reverberated through my body. But I didn't have time to think or react or swing or even scream —

Shit got desperate so fast.

He picked me up by my throat. I couldn't do anything but swing flailing punches at his chest and kick his shins. He barely noticed my weak-ass pummels as he stared blearily down at my bare legs.

Then he shoved me hard onto the stone floor. The back of my head struck the hard cold ground, and my hand reflexively went to the back of my head. Dazed, I thought, *concussion*, but also, I couldn't think about the pain, the dizzy, the dark, because he dove down on me crushing me under his weight. His forearm pressed across my throat. His free hand prying open my kicking, struggling legs.

He spoke again, a bark like an order I didn't understand.

I screeched out, "I'm with Magnus, Magnus Campbell!"

He paused for a millisecond. "You art a Brit," then continued groping violently between my legs.

I screamed as his hand ripped my panties away from my body and fumbled up the fabric of his kilt. He shoved his knee up, parting mine, as I begged, "Magnus Campbell." I kicked, trying to keep him away.

"Magnus Campbell is verra auld." He shoved my legs aside, pressing further on my throat, breathing hard in my ears, pushing himself up and closer.

"No, stop please, the young Magnus." I flailed weakly at the side of his arms, but breathing was difficult, and I was trying to clamp down with every internal muscle to keep him out.

"Young Magnus is nae here anymore." He pushed against me up hard and in and I screamed until the arm crushed my breath from my throat and—

"Nae!" Magnus's voice was grim and loud and terrible and close. "Cousin, I will cut ye, ear to ear if ye touch her." Magnus had his knife at the man's throat, as the man convulsed and lifted off my body. The forearm that had been stealing my breath pulled away from my throat, the hips that had been crushing me pulled away from my pelvis. Then the monster withdrew from between my legs last of all.

I clutched the cloak around my body, as my Magnus stood holding the man by a clutch of hair. Roaring in Gaelic, he brought his knee up hard into the man's stomach, doubling him over. He slammed a knee up squarely into his nose, probably breaking it, and then Magnus was everywhere fists and knees, punching, swinging, pummeling the man, beating him senseless with his bare hands.

The older woman from the kitchen stood in the doorway wringing her hands. She yelled loudly in Gaelic.

Magnus turned on her, "I asked ye tae watch over the lady."

She spoke in English, "I dinna hear him approach, but thee canna kill him, Master Magnus. Tis too much trouble for thee."

Magnus stopped cold, glaring into the pummeled face of the man, bloodied and mangled. He bellowed, "That is my wife."

He climbed to his feet and grabbing the man by his hair dragged him to his knees. "Beg her forgiveness." Magnus's voice was terrible, cold and scary.

The man spoke quietly in words I didn't understand.

Magnus shook him by the hair roots. "Beg for it, in English!"

"My apologies, Madame."

"Madame Campbell, dost ye want me tae spare his life?"

I nodded quickly and looked away.

Magnus leaned over to look in the man's face. "Cousin, this lady, that you have injured, Madame Campbell, has spared your life this day. Will ye touch her again?"

"Nae, nocht."

Magnus dropped the man's hair allowing him to slump to the ground. He thrust his blade to the man's throat. "You will nae look upon her again, or I will kill ye. Dost ye understand my words and meanin'?"

"Aye, Magnus."

"You may leave."

The man heaved himself up struggling with his footing. Blood smeared his face. He wobbled and weaved as he made it to the door and through to the kitchen. The older woman left too.

I clutched my cloak around myself on the cold hard ground.

My husband remained crouched where he had been staring into the man's eyes. Immobile. Ragged breaths heaved his shoulders. He dropped down to sitting, his back to me, elbows on his knees. He held his knife in his hands.

His breaths were bullish, through his nose, furiously loud. His anger had flooded so high, I could hear him attempt to squelch it under.

He asked, still turned away, his voice even, measured, and low, "Did he hurt ye?"

I felt the back of my head. It was a mean bump but probably fine. My throat hurt, but — "Not too bad."

He sat quietly for long terrible angry moments. "I canna get on top of it." He clutched his chest.

I nodded, staring up at the ceiling. I was having trouble with my breaths too.

"Was he inside ye, Kaitlyn?"

I shook my head, but he couldn't see me and I couldn't bring myself to lie. "Not entire—"

"Daena say it." He shook his head and growled, a sound low and desperate and guttural. "I canna let him have ye."

Then he turned, yanked my cloak aside, and climbed on me. He shoved his hips up against my body and pushed himself inside me with another growl and another and another. His head was down by my shoulder, growling and grunting, slamming into me over and over. I bit into his shoulder to hold my cries. And held on, meeting his desperate force with my own counter force, until finally, with a final blow and a shuddering groan, he collapsed down, spent, done.

His breath continued ragged but not violent anymore. I focused on the spot on his shoulder where I had been biting and fell away. My arms dropped to the cloak-draped ground. It was freezing cold on this stone floor.

He raised up to his knees and stared down at me spread-eagled before him. Then he took my hand and pulled me to standing before him. He raised my sundress a little and made a small sad adjustment of my tiny, little, now torn-to-rags, panties, trying to set them to rights.

Then he rested his hands on my hips, dropped his forehead to my belly, and with his head down, face pressed into my stomach, he cried. Hugging my hips, quietly, his shoulders shaking.

I held onto the back of his head until he was done.

"I am sorry for it Kaitlyn."

I was shivering cold through to my core. The kind of cold that might never leave me. Soul cold. Bitter cold. Iced hard through.

"I know."

"I had tae. I canna let him have ye. I had tae make ye mine again."

I took a deep breath trying to get any kind of warmth into my body. "I understand why you did it, but you need to get your fucking hands off of me." I pushed his hands down my hips and away.

He sat for a moment looking down at the ground before him while I stared at the back wall. Then he rose and said, "I'll take ye tae our room."

CHAPTER 18

*M*agnus led me up a back stairwell, down wide tapestry-hung halls, and through bare stone-walled hallways. I guessed we were on the third floor, and it was dark, too dark to make out what i was seeing. I just followed. Oh, and it was freezing cold.

He pushed open a heavy wooden door and spoke briefly with a young woman who had been tending a hearth. She bowed a bit as she scooted past me to leave.

I headed straight for the fire to warm my hands. I was shaking to my core — from the temperatures and fear. My nerves were jangled past breaking. I kind of wondered if I might go a little psychotic because this was terrifying. I had been here for about eight hours and my husband hated me. I had been sexually assaulted, watched my husband beat a man, and then I was anger-banged by Magnus and—

I burst into tears. Clutching my cloak, a hand on my mouth — rending my cloth and twisting my skin — what the fuck was I doing here? I wanted to go back, but it was so awful. I didn't want to. And what was to be done — what would I do? I sank onto a settee, wrapped all around my legs in a ball, and cried.

And I was cold to my core freezing.

Plus my whole area between my legs hurt like hell because I had been wearing tiny panties and a sundress when I rode a horse for hours in the freezing cold. Plus I was attacked and—

I cried longer until I wondered if I might never stop.

Magnus grabbed a large wool blanket from the bed, covered me with it, and tucked it around me. It was scratchy. Then he knelt in front of my chair and reached for my hand jarring me back to reality. I snatched my hand away.

He slumped to the ground, leaned on my settee, and watched me quietly.

I pulled the cloak around my head and the blanket up to my eyes.

"Dost ye remember the night we decided tae be married?"

I nodded. My eyes focused on the deep darkness under the blanket. I didn't look at Magnus; I didn't know if I could ever look at him again. I was so full of anger or fear or shame or — all of it, every bit of every terrible horrible feeling.

"I promised ye I would be better as time goes on. And I have broken that promise tae ye. I know, I hear it in your cries. I am afeared ye will nae forgive me, and I beg of ye tae try."

I sniffled. "You said that I was like the North Star and you would follow me." I shook, even with the wool blanket, even with the fire close by.

"Mo reul-iuil, I call ye, and I mean it. I have just lost my way."

"You said that and bunch of other romantic stuff, but you have been barely speaking to me the whole time we've been here. And it's scary. And it hurt. And you've just been grumbling at me. And you left me alone. And that guy. And then you—" I sobbed into my knees. "I think you may have broken my heart."

"I know. I have sworn tae protect ye and take care of ye and I will make good on it."

He rose up on his knees and stroked a finger under each of my eyes to wipe my tears.

I shook his hands away.

"Talk tae me, Kaitlyn, please."

"No, you can't tell me not to say anything — to not argue and to obey and to be good and be quiet — and then beg me to tell you what's wrong. That's not the way this works."

"I am new tae this, mo reul-iuil. Please allow me tae begin again."

I sat with my jaw set. "My head hurts. I'm super thirsty. Can you get me some water?"

"I dinna ken tis water in the room." He stood and checked the small table to the side. "There is wine?"

I sighed. "Okay."

He brought me a cup with wine in it. I drank it down and swiped my hand across my lips to wipe them. "Thanks."

"Will you forgive me, mo ghradh?"

"Remind me what 'mo gra' means?"

"It means my own love."

"See, that's not fair, to be mad at me all day and then think you can call me something in Gaelic so I'll forgive you. And why were you mad? Because I didn't obey you. Well you didn't protect me. So we both let each other down. We can both be furious with each other."

"I am nae angry with ye Kaitlyn, nae anymore."

"Because you feel bad about what happened to me. Maybe you only feel it because I'm damaged now — well guess what? I feel really damaged. I feel completely broken. And totally alone."

He looked in my eyes. His were full of fear, but mine had grown hard. I had grown even more furious the more I talked about it. We sat in silence.

Finally I asked, "What are we going to do?"

"I am going tae beg ye tae forgive—"

"No, I mean, now, for dinner, what do we do next?"

"I have asked for a dress for ye. Tis on the bed. And we must dine in the great hall tonight. My Uncle Baldie is off traveling. So I am left tae deal with the Earl directly. I must ask him tae give me men tae return tae Talsworth Castle tae find Lady Mairead."

"When you're there you'll need to find both the vessels, the one that Lord Delapointe has and the one that Lady Mairead has hidden."

"Tis a verra delicate matter, usually Baldie would arrange things for me. He is Sean's uncle and likes me verra much. But the situation with the Earl is far more delicate. He daena like me much. And Lady Mairead has caused him much trouble."

"So you think he will give you men?"

"Aye, twill take some negotiating, but Lady Mairead is his sister and she has been ill-used by her husband. I have been held there and whipped. I dinna ken the Earl will accept the challenge tae his power."

I said, "Then you and these other men will walk up to the Castle Talsworth and tell them you demand to see Lady Mairead?"

"I imagine twill be verra more dangerous than that."

"Me too."

"You will need a history. I was planning it while we rode today. You are my wife, Kaitlyn Sheffield. Your father is stationed in the West Indies, where ye were raised. Tis why ye speak so strange."

I gave him a half-hearted chuckle.

"I met ye in London and married ye just afore I was captured by Lord Delapointe." He looked worried but I couldn't rally any empathy.

I closed my eyes. "I'll make sure to just keep my mouth closed."

"Kaitlyn—"

I opened my eyes. "C'mon Magnus, be truthful. Do you want me to talk or sit silent and let you talk? Because I know which you want, so out with it."

Magnus looked at me with a plead in his eyes. "Twould be better if ye were quiet. Tis true, but not the—"

"In 2017 you galavanted around town in a kilt, carrying a sword, talking to anyone. Zach guessed, and you didn't worry about it. No one told you you couldn't."

"Here every man has a sword, and they are watchin' every other man for a weakness. I have nae lived long, but still I have killed men. Tis a different history, Kaitlyn, and ye know tis true if ye think on it." He shook his head slowly with a tiny bit of a smile. "And I dinna galavant. You make me seem silly. I believe I looked rather dignified on my horse, Sunny."

I humphed. "Whatever, you get my point. And I'm still furious at you. You might be right that Scotland in the 18th century, is more dangerous than Florida in 2017. And yeah, I have a bruise on my face that proves it, so I'll be quiet and let you talk. But I won't be happy about it."

Magnus asked, "So ye will hate me then?"

"Yes. This morning you said what I did was unforgivable. So we're even."

"If you hate me what will ye do?"

"I'll go back to 2017. First chance."

Very quietly Magnus asked, "If you go with the vessel what happens if I canna find another one?"

I chewed my lip. "I guess you don't get to ever come."

"You would leave me forever?"

I pulled the blanket up to my cheeks. "Maybe."

"What if I winna give ye the vessel?"

It had grown dark outside, casting our room into even deeper darkness, The firelight flickered on his cheek. The only part of the room I could see, his jawline. It didn't seem fair. "You would keep me here, against my will?"

He gave me a sad smile. "Maybe."

"Fine, I don't need you. I'm industrious and capable. I'll just stay, but not with you."

"And what would ye do?"

"I will take a horse, ride as far away as I can, and live in a little cottage somewhere. Just making crepes and keeping chickens or something."

"You hate me so much ye would become a horse thief and grow old alone in the forest?"

"I won't be alone, I'll have thirty kittens."

"How would ye feed them all?"

I chuckled a bit, beginning to feel a little warmer. "You heard me, I'll make crepes. Lots of crepes. With Nutella."

He raised his brow with a laugh. "You are verra beautiful. I winna be able tae stay away. I will have a tent just outside your house. I will live there in the cold and protect ye every day of my life."

I rolled my eyes.

He looked down at his hands. "When we were downstairs, I asked ye if I should kill him. I wanted tae. If ye had said, "Aye," I would have slit his throat. It would have been verra bad for me, but I wanted tae kill him. You said tae spare his life though, and I listened tae ye. If ye command it I will honor your word. I just ask ye tae honor mine."

"You would have killed him for me?"

"Och aye, Kaitlyn Campbell, on one word. I would have been hung for it, but twould have been a willing trade. I am grateful for your wisdom in the matter."

I sighed again, deeply. I still felt so wronged, but I also felt a bit better listening to the rumbling voice of my husband. "You would really live in a tent outside my forest cottage?"

"I would hunt for food for ye and leave it on your doorstep."

"Food?"

"Like rabbits and deer."

"I'm not sharing the Nutella though."

"I would rather have vanilla ice cream. I miss Chef Zach terribly."

"Me too. And I don't know how to cook a rabbit. It sounds complicated. I suppose it's a terrible plan." The darkness of the room made the prospect of food seem hopeful. I was hungry. I flung back the rough blanket and went and shivered near the bed looking down at the pile of dress that also looked very complicated.

In the mound of fabric there was a long white linen dress with a scooped neckline. I guessed that was an underdress, but — without turning I asked, "Is this what I put on first?"

"Aye."

I slipped off my filthy sundress. "Don't look over here."

He turned back to the fire.

"What about underwear, panties, whatever — bloomers?"

"'Tis nae done."

I sighed and wiggled the white chemise down over my body. Then I dropped my torn, filthy panties to the ground. They had been a beautiful vintage-looking gray lace. I bought them because they looked old-fashioned and I thought Magnus would appreciate that, but now, beside this gigantic pile of thick, wool clothing, they looked much newer. Even torn they looked like they were from a different century altogether. Showed what I knew.

"Please daena hate me anymore."

I humphed, lifting a very, very, heavy deep green skirt up and stepping into it. I twisted it around looking for a zipper, button, string at the top, or anything.

Magnus said, "You need tae use the belt."

I looped the leather strap around the top of the skirt and threaded the end through a buckle. The rest of the pile had what looked like a jacket and piles of cloth I didn't know what to do with. . . I was quite cold and growing frustrated. "Do you know how to do this?"

He rose and came to the bed. "I have never dressed a woman afore but—"

I stood stoically while he unloosed the belt, clutched the skirt, and held the jacket for me. I slipped my arms into the sleeves. We tucked the skirt up into it, and he began lacing it in the back.

He cinched it all tight and then rounded me to check the front. "Och, see, I dinna do it well. The front should hold your breasts up more." He unloosed the back.

I pushed my breasts up so my cleavage looked fantastic, and he tightened the back again. He returned to the pile and picked up a shawl, and draped it across my back, hanging down in the front, and lastly, he added the belt around my middle cinched tight to hold it all in place.

His hands paused at my bodice-tightened waist. "Tis a beautiful look on ye, Kaitlyn." He placed his forehead on mine. "I am verra sorry for my words and actions on this day. I will make it up tae ye, please give me the chance."

I reached out and touched his arm and nodded my forehead against his lips.

"You will?"

"Yes, I will forgive you, eventually."

"Thank ye, Kaitlyn. Tis your second pardon of the day that has saved my life." He kissed me on my forehead and then held me at arm's length admiring me in my dress.

I said, "Now that I'm dressed. I desperately need to use the bathroom, so far it's been outdoors?"

"Tis much the same." He strode to the corner of the room and swept his arm out to show me a porcelain piece shaped much like a sauce pan. "Your chamber pot."

I stood beside him and looked down on it. "I think I'll need more information."

Magnus mimed how I would lift my skirts and crouch above it, and we laughed, remembering the night I showed him how to use a toilet in 2017. Though the modern toilets had a lot more complications. This was really a lot like peeing outdoors without the getting-to-walk-away afterwards.

While I peed he joked, "Tis much like home, just without the frosted glass door between us."

"And the toilet seat and the paper and the flusher and the..." I wiggled my hips to dry myself. "This sucks."

Magnus grinned, "Wait until ye try the food."

I groaned.

"You will ken that when I am here without ye I am killin' m'self tryin' tae return."

"Yeah, I get that. I understand a lot more now. Also, I was thinking we need a word we can use between us. One that will mean stop, no, I disagree. So I can use it without arguing with you in front of the Earl. It would mean, 'wait, let's discuss this.' Like a safe word."

"A safe word?"

"Yes, um, in sex, um, couples have a 'safe word.' It means 'stop' if things get too wild, too painful or scary or something."

Magnus blinked down at me. "Your explanation needs more explanation."

I blushed to my hairline. "I haven't ever needed one, but if you're playing around with bondage or um, something, you might say 'no' but not mean it. You and your partner have a word that means 'no, *really*.'"

"Our word is 'refrigerator.' But bondage, you have never said this — tis something that is done?"

"I think so, yes."

He blinked a couple of times.

"Are you okay Magnus?"

"I am speechless as I consider this new — husbands and wives do this?"

"Sometimes, I guess, if they want. Magnus, I'm so hungry. Our safe word is 'refrigerator'?"

"Och aye, refrigerator. Speaking of which, we ought tae descend tae the great hall tae eat." He grabbed a candle from a table and took my hand.

CHAPTER 19

*a*t the doorway I faltered. It was pitch black like I had suddenly gone completely blind. He held the flickering candle closer to my face. "Can ye see?"

I shook my head.

He put his elbow in front of my chest and I wrapped my hands around it. I found myself alternating between wild panic trying to get my eyes to adjust, and staring at the tiny flickering flame of the candle, wishing it would actually light up the space.

"Can you see?" I asked.

"Och aye, tis quite dark, but I can see." I gave up the struggle and just stared down at where my feet ought to be, concentrating on making out their form. I clutched Magnus's arm as he led me down the dark hallway, down a winding staircase, down another equally dark hallway. This one though had a couple of torches burning along the wall, giving off a tiny bit of light. It helpfully added to our candle's faint flicker a tiny bit. Our shadows spilled behind us.

We descended another stair and when we reached the floors

below there was more ambient light. Torches lined the walls. The rooms opened up. There were windows, albeit small, lining one side. It was still faint and shadowy, but not outright terrifying.

We entered one long wide hall. Tapestries lined the right side; large paintings lined the left. Long drapes covered the windows. Woven rugs covered the floor. This room also had some furniture. Chairs and the occasional table stood at points along the passage. The ceilings swept very high. Each noise seemed amplified. Our footsteps echoed.

The entire place smelled of mold and dust but also fire and wax and herbs and flowers. It was a lovely smell, deep and rich. We passed a window, and I realized that it had begun to rain, dark, driving, wet and probably cold. But I was warm finally, grateful to be inside an eighteenth century castle.

Me. Inside an eighteenth century castle. And not as a tourist.

I held Magnus's arm tighter. It was very quiet except for the rain's staccato on the glass of the windows.

The long room held more decorations as we walked along it. The furniture and tapestries became more ornate. There were beautifully carved tables and chairs and many large paintings. We passed through one final doorway into a room that had paintings lining both walls, wallpaper, sculptures through the middle, and ornately carved cornices.

"Oooh," I tried to make out the ceiling, there were more candles and torches, but still it was difficult to see beyond about ten feet.

"Tomorrow I'll shew ye this room. Tis a beautiful collection. The Earl plans tae rebuild the whole castle in a newer style. He thinks this one is too brutish and cold."

Halfway down the wall, two large doors stood ajar, and whatever was happening inside spilled out toward us — dancing firelight, loud jovial voices, and twanging music.

"I will have tae do and say some things tae the Earl— he is verra political, always slippery about his plans."

"No worries, I can improv."

He looked at me with his brow drawn.

"I mean, I'll let you do the talking."

"Och aye, and ye are ready tae meet some of my family?"

CHAPTER 20

The great hall looked exactly like its name a long hallway grown huge. The length was three times as long as it was wide. The beautiful ornate ceiling soared above us, making me feel tiny and insignificant. And though the assembled party numbered over forty, the crowd was dwarfed by the scale of the walls. One very long table ran down the expanse of it, lined on each side by chairs full of people, young and old. They were loudly talking and in the cavernous room it was very loud. Many servers bustled around carrying platters, covered in dishes and pitchers.

Magnus grasped my hand under his arm and set his sights on the head of the table. He pulled me toward it down the side of the room.

Mine was a long nervous approach. I tried to keep my eyes down, but there were so many odd faces turned our direction. As we passed through the room, diners ceased talking, and stopped eating mid-bite. They twisted in their chairs to see us. They stared and whispered as our passage caused a ripple effect of silence from one end to the other.

We arrived and Magnus pulled to a stop and stood, head bowed. I dropped my head as well. At the table sat a man in one of those historical founding-father-style long flowing wigs that I never ever thought I would see on a person. He was wearing makeup. His skin was pale white, his eyebrows arched dark, rouge circles on his cheeks. His features, similar to Lady Mairead, looked pinched and twisted on him. He ignored us, continuing to speak with the woman to his right. She was occasionally glancing up at us, but he remained indifferent.

After a moment Magnus cleared his throat. I remained clutching his arm, staring down at the floor. Under the tablecloth there were crumbs, a half-eaten potato, and a couple of bones, about chicken leg size.

After a moment, the man turned in an affected motion that seemed to say, *As important as I am I had not noticed you there.* He sized Magnus up, his eyes flicked toward me, then quickly away. "Ah, the young Magnus, home from your travels?"

"Aye, Lord Breadalbane, I am home. I wish tae present my wife, Madame Kaitlyn Campbell."

"Ah!" The Earl's eyes flitted down the table to where my attacker sat, staring at his dinner plate, his face black blue and swollen. "Welcome Madame Campbell, and where do ye hail from? You will forgive me, I had nae heard young Magnus had taken a wife."

"It's a pleasure to meet you. My former name is Kaitlyn Sheffield—"

He interrupted to say, "You are a Brit?"

His brow raised and his eyes drew away from me and leveled on Magnus while I answered, "Yes, though I have lived my entire life in the West Indies."

He leaned back nodding. "Och aye, the sugar! I have developed a taste for it, twill be good tae have a connection tae the sugar trade in the family I think." He laughed, a practiced laugh, and looked up and down the table for general agreement. "And how are you enjoying the visit tae my castle so far?"

He leveled his gaze on Magnus while waiting for my answer.

I felt Magnus's muscles tighten. His energy shifted, his will engaged.

I said, "It has been—"

Magnus interrupted me. His jaw set, his eyes stormed over. "Lord Breadalbane, I canna sit at this table until my cousin has been made tae vacate his chair. I winna share a table with him."

Everyone turned to look at the man who attacked me. The sight of him made me shake with fear.

He stared straight ahead chewing slowly.

Magnus watched the Earl, refusing to look away.

The Earl said, "Ah, so this is the history of your ugly maw, Ewan. You said ye fell down drunk."

Everyone twittered amusedly.

"He has attempted tae fall down drunk upon my wife."

The Earl's eyes rested on my bruised cheek. "Och aye, tis a wonder you dinna kill him young Magnus."

"Madame Campbell has asked him tae be spared. But—" Magnus turned to Ewan and banged his fist on the table jostling the china and glassware. His voice raising dangerously high. "His eyes winna quit looking at her." He turned back to the Earl. "Lord Breadalbane, I insist he must nae remain at this table or the Madame Campbell and I will return tae our rooms and leave on the morrow."

The Earl put his hands out placatingly. "Now now, we'll have none of that. Madame Campbell is welcome here and has my promise nae harm will come tae her. You feel affronted, young Magnus?" He leaned forward and bellowed down the table. "Ewan, didst ye know that Madame Campbell was the wife of your cousin?"

He said sullenly, "Nae."

"See, Magnus, tis a misunderstanding. Twill nae happen again. Though I can see ye are raring tae fight. In the service of peace within my great hall I will arrange a better seating." He looked back down at Ewan. "I wish ye to move, Ewan. Take a seat farther down the table."

Ewan slammed back his chair, yanked his plate and drink and stormed off to another chair.

"See, young Magnus, sit here," He waved a finger and a man and a woman vacated the seats closest to the Earl, giving them over to us. "Have a drink and some food and tell me what has happened to your mother."

CHAPTER 21

$\mathcal{T}$he food was passable. Probably because it was so necessary. Meaty and filling, though really seriously needing some spice, or sauce, or sweetness. And some vegetables. The dessert was much like the meal — not sweet. But I hadn't eaten in a day. Or make that centuries. I was ravenous enough to have eaten a horse. Lamb would do. A pudding would do for dessert. Lots and lots of beer because I was so crazy thirsty.

It was hard to focus on the discussion between Magnus and the Earl. Magnus also spoke to many other men who came up, clapped him on the shoulder, and spoke long and boisterously to him about battles or — really I had no idea what they were talking about. Forced to guess it was all about fighting. Then as soon as they left Magnus and the Earl returned to speaking directly to each other. My hearing was still wonky. Their voices were just a bit too low. My heartbeat and breathing were just a bit too loud. My senses were all jangled. My nerves weren't as jangled though, by degrees — the effect of the beer.

I overheard the Earl say, "You have heard His Royal Highness, King William, has passed?"

Magnus's face clouded over, he shook his head. "Nae I haena heard."

The Earl studied Magnus's face, then asked, "I believe you spent much time at court, were you friendly to the King?"

Magnus's jaw clenched. "I never met His Royal Highness, I was never presented at court." I watched the side of Magnus's face. He was lying to the Earl, but I didn't know why.

"So you don't have an opinion on succession young Magnus?"

"Nae, my opinion lies with you, my grace, with my cousins and my family."

"Ah, well said, but understand your family and your country lies divided about a great many things."

The Earl and Magnus leaned closer and discussed the 'many things' for longer until finally Magnus leaned back with a grim look on his face. The Earl turned away and rejoined his former conversation with the woman on his right.

"What happened? He wouldn't give you any men?"

"He has said he canna spare them. There are uprisings and rebellions in every quarter and he needs his armies. He will give me two men tae accompany me tae Talsworth—"

"But last time you were there you were held a prisoner. You'll be captured."

"Aye. I might be able tae send one of the men inside, but if I am captured, I can't see that will do me any good." He shrugged. "Though at least I would be on the inside."

"No, no, that's not—" I fumed trying to imagine a better plan than this. I could think of three right off my head:

One, call Lord Delapointe by phone and tell him to release Lady Mairead immediately.

Two, call the police.

Three, fly planes over and drop bombs until he surrenders.

None of those would— "Are the men good, that will be traveling with you?"

His eyes flitted to mine nervously. "I have picked them."

"So they're good? Who is it?"

"My brother, Sean, and another cousin. They are good enough."

I stewed quietly. "And I'll be here, alone, six hours away while you're gone?"

"Nae, twould be best for ye tae be back home."

"No. Now that it's so much harder to do this, I won't leave with the only vessel we have. I won't. We both go together or we go when we have two vessels in our possession. That's the only way. It can't be too hard to see Lady Mairead. You just — the Earl should go with you and take a band of men. He should demand a conversation with her." I glanced up and despite our whispers the Earl was listening to our discussion. "Lord Breadalbane—" I spoke across Magnus.

He turned with a broad, well-practiced smile on his face. "Dear niece, your opinion differs from mine?"

"It does, I mean, I don't want to overstep — I understand you have difficulties raising enough men for Magnus, but to send him with only two men means he will probably be captured again, and then Lord Delapointe would be holding your sister and your nephew, it seems —"

Magnus said, "Kaitlyn."

I clamped my lips between my teeth.

The Earl looked from me to Magnus. "I would like for my new niece to finish, young Magnus."

Magnus sighed.

I said, "Magnus was beaten. I'm afraid if he goes anywhere near the castle he will not come out again."

"Tis true?"

"Aye, he held me captive for a time."

I finished. "His back still has whip marks."

Lord Breadalbane made a sound like a tsk tsk. "You did see your mother there, young Magnus?"

"Nae."

"So Lord Delapointe wants your capture. You dinna mention this afore." The Earl gestured to have his beer filled again and waved toward my half-full glass too. "Tis more complicated. I have heard nocht of Lady Mairead in many weeks."

Magnus said, "I saw her about a month ago, she spoke tae me of some danger tae her."

The Earl sighed and seemed about to give up the conversation altogether. I had to act. "What if I went?"

The Earl and Magnus both directed their focus to me.

"I could go to the castle—"

Magnus said, "Kaitlyn..."

"What if I told Lord Delapointe that Magnus is missing, and I need to speak to Lady Mairead about his disappearance?" I spoke faster because Magnus's expression turned sharp. "If you went, Lord Breadalbane, as my escort, he would have to answer us."

Magnus mouthed, "Refrigerator."

The Earl raised his brow. "I would attend you?"

"Yes, it would raise no suspicions if the uncle and wife of Magnus Campbell were to appear to ask about him. Why shouldn't we ask to speak to Lady Mairead?"

Magnus's eyes grew wide. "Refrigerator."

I turned a fierce eye on Magnus, and said, "Refrigerator," in return. To the Earl I finished, "And then we would learn if Lady Mairead is okay."

The Earl seemed amused about our facial expressions and back and forth, "Froigrator?"

"Tis an expression in the West Indies. It means, 'I disagree *vehemently.*'" Magnus's jaw was hard, his gaze forceful.

The Earl said, "I believe Madame Campbell's idea has

some merit. Twould take us just a couple of days tae accomplish. I would take six men. Would ye want tae attend us, Magnus?"

Magnus grumbled, "Och aye, if Kaitlyn is going I will attend her. Though I am nae convinced this is—"

The Earl waved him away with a hand. "We are decided. I suppose if Madame Campbell travels with us, you winna want Ewan?"

I glanced sharply at Magnus.

He said, "I asked tae take Ewan with me so ye winna have tae see him while I was away."

I gulped at the idea of Magnus traveling with Ewan; someone would end up dead for sure. Possibly everyone. He was still glaring at us from his place at the far end of the table. I clutched Magnus's hand. Settled in my mind that my idea was the best plan.

The Earl said, "The rain will clear tomorrow morning. We will ride just after dawn and arrive before dark." He turned away to speak again with the woman to his right.

Magnus urgently whispered, "Nae Kaitlyn, ye canna go in there. I winna be with you. I winna be able tae protect you. You expect me tae watch ye go into Delapointe's castle without me? He is—"

I clutched his fingers, and whispered "Magnus, think about it — you're waiting just outside. I go in with the Earl, under his protection. We're surrounded by men. I see Lady Mairead and she tells me everything she knows about the location of the other two boxes. I leave, meet you outside, and we decide what to do next."

Magnus scowled. "I suppose ye could have the vessel with you. If anything happened ye could return tae your time."

"No, you'd have the vessel. If something happens, you storm the castle and rescue me. We jump together. That's the thing

Magnus. We only have one vessel right now. I'm not jumping without you; I might never see you again."

He sat quietly looking around the great hall. I scanned the room too, the tapestry across from my seat, the carved wall, and especially people, the faces down the table. Many looking like relatives of Lady Mairead. The men and women were all dressed, layers of clothes, nicer than my own, hair done. The servants were bustling around. The noise had grown louder as the night became later. Beer was passed around the tables. A musician played a stringed instrument behind us.

As if he read my thoughts Magnus said, "Tis nae Food Fighters."

I laughed. "It's hard to be mad at you when you're so helpless. You can't even get the band's name right. You need me so desperately."

"I do, I am a desperate man without ye." He nodded looking out over the hall. "Okay Kaitlyn, I agree. And if we only have one vessel, we will jump together."

"Thank you."

"But, if you find a second vessel at the castle. If ye can get your hands on it, steal it, take it back home. I will get tae ye."

"Okay, it's a deal."

He clasped my hand, and we watched the diners for a few minutes. Finally Magnus's brother, Sean, entered the room. He rushed us and swept Magnus up into a gigantic bear hug. Magnus and Sean banged each other's shoulders. Their hulking masses exclaiming and battering each other happily, until Magnus flinched painfully. "I have an injury brother, tis—"

Sean deftly twisted Magnus and yanked the back of his shirt to forcefully look inside the neck. "What has happened to ye Mags?"

I chuckled, remembering James calling Magnus 'Mags' too.

"I have had a run in with Lady Mairead's husband."

"Och, well, tis only a scratch."

Magnus laughed and introduced me. Sean exclaimed, "Kaitlyn, sister!" And hugged me so tightly I wondered if a rib might break. Magnus asked after his sister, Lizabeth, who happened to be off traveling with their Uncle Baldie.

Then Sean was told about our errand the following morning. His voice boomed. "So we must rescue mum again, fine, though I wish she would make a better choice of husbands."

Magnus laughed, "Her newest one seems tae be the most dangerous of the lot."

Sean said, "True. We'll catch up tomorrow, Mags, on our ride. I need to get some food in me in the meantime. And speaking of better choices, ye needs be careful. Ye are making enemies of your cousins, I hear. I will need tae mend the bonds and I daena want tae work so hard."

"You heard then?"

"The whole castle heard. Cousin Ewan is much favored by the Earl. I am grateful ye spared his life or I might be attending a hanging tomorrow instead of an easy visit with mum."

They hugged again before Sean left to sit at a seat at the far end of the table. Another group of men came up to speak to Magnus. He introduced me to what seemed like the hundredth person.

The Earl stood and made a speech, mostly Gaelic. It was followed by cheers. Cups were raised in our direction. My name was said, so I blushed though I had no idea what was being said about me. I drank more beer, feeling quite tipsy and comfortable for the first time in hours.

Magnus whispered, "Chef Zach right now is scooping vanilla for Emma."

"Ah, but see, she is fond of chocolate fudge with ribbons of marshmallow through it. Plus she is pregnant. She probably wants pickles or something with it."

"Pickles? With ice cream?" He looked outraged, but then laughed. "Well, I will try anything once."

We both gestured for another beer and drank it, whispering to each other and laughing at inside jokes.

"I would like tae have a baby with ye Kaitlyn."

"I'd prefer to have babies in my century than yours."

He rubbed his hand along the back of mine. "Would ye like tae go upstairs?"

I glanced across the room. Ewan was glaring at us. It had only been about six hours since he had his forearm across my throat. Only about four hours since I had been furious with my husband and yes, the food and beer had helped my mood, but I didn't feel loving or sexy yet. Not when my head still ached from the punch and when it hit the stone floor. "I'm not in the mood for anything Magnus. I'm still... I need some sleep and time to get back there."

He kissed my fingers with a nod. He leaned to the Earl's ear and told him we were retiring to our quarters, and then we walked the long dark corridors back to our bedroom.

CHAPTER 22

irst Magnus had to stoke and build the fire anew because our room was freezing. It felt like it was about ten degrees Fahrenheit. I wrapped myself in the scratchy wool blanket on the settee and waited for Magnus to help me untie the binding, too-tight bodice. As soon as Magnus finished with the fire, he unlaced the strings so I could shimmy out of it tossing it to the floor.

I scrabbled through my bag for more lip balm and smeared it on my lips. "Ah, this is heaven, all the comforts of home."

I returned to the settee in front of the fire and Magnus put his arm out for me to curl under. "We should stay here until we are warm enough tae go tae the bed. The heat barely moves from this spot."

I watched the firelight dance and felt held strong and comfortable by my husband. I had never watched a fire burn while in his arms. It was another first. And I reminded myself that these were all firsts; we were still so new to each other, trying to figure it out.

"What are ye thinking of?"

"How this is our honeymoon. The trip we would take after we're married, to celebrate."

His voice was quiet and rumbling through the darkness. "Tis too heartrending tae be a celebration."

"It's an adventure, that might be a good start too."

"Ah." He nudged my head with his shoulder so he could look down into my eyes. "Tis the first thing ye have said that truly sounds like ye have forgiven me."

I tightened my hold around his chest. "I have, I'm just... I still feel wounded. Rubbed raw. I just need you to hold me right now."

He kissed my forehead and we laid there until I fell asleep in his arms.

CHAPTER 23

I woke up a few hours later, discombobulated, uncertain, confused, trying to get my eyes to adjust to the complete darkness of the room. Oh, it came to me with a jolt — I was in an eighteenth century castle. My whole body ached, time jumping, horse riding, rape, all had worked on my last nerve, muscle, sinew. Magnus had at some time in the night moved me to the bed. Plus this bed was not right — the mattress felt like it was stuffed with a handful of feathers wrapped under heavy linen. Like an air mattress gone soft. It fluffed in a few places, but not where I needed it, leaving me on flat wood planks.

There was a rustling sound on the floor.

My body tightened. I listened. There was definitely something in the room with us. I whispered, "Magnus? Magnus!" I pushed against his chest to wake him.

"Huh?"

"Magnus, something's in our room. Over there." I tucked behind his chest as he turned to peer toward it.

He finally said, "Tis a rat, over near the fireplace." He started laughing. "Tis nothing, just a verminous animal in our bed quarters m'lady." He laughed harder.

I laughed too, holding him around the middle.

"Rats, fleas, bedbugs, nothing but the best for ye," he said, laughing still.

"Bed bugs?" I tucked even closer to his chest. "Rats — what do you suppose it's doing over there?"

He listened. "Did you have any food in your bag?"

"No, god, it's in my bag, ew."

"Tis a good distraction, will keep him from our bed."

"Magnus! Our bed, it might come in our bed?" I wrapped tighter around his body. "I need my phone to call the exterminator. Can you ask the rat to drag my bag over here?"

He laughed harder. "Why does my wife believe I can converse with rats?"

"I'm assuming they are Gaelic rats. In Florida if a cockroach walked through our house at night I would be the one asking it to bring me things. Okay wait, that's bullshit, cockroaches are worse than rats."

"Rats have teeth, my dear Kaitlyn, and they daena speak Gaelic. They speak evil."

Tiny rat footsteps scurried away.

I giggled. "You hurt its feelings."

Magnus said, "More likely, whatever they were searching for they are done with."

"What could it have been. . . the only thing I had in there was my — oh no, my Burt's Bees lip balm? Could they, would they? My lips will fall off my face."

"Och aye, tis what gives ye the taste of peppermint and honey? Two of the favorite foods of rats. I think ye may be done with the lip balm, mo reul-iuil." His fingers traced up and down my arm. We were snuggled under a thick linen cloth. The scratchy wool blanket was spread on top of that, and then a fur that might have been a bear or something else big and too awful to imagine. Heavy layers. His fingers trailed to my chin and pulled it up, meeting my lips with his.

He kissed me long and deep. His fingers tracing up and down my arms and then caressing along my side and pulling my leg across his waist. The dark was near total, another first for us. In our room at home we mostly kept the windows unshaded, the glow of the moon giving our room an ambient light.

Here it was just pitch black, complete. So my other senses took over. The sound of my heartbeat and breath rang in my ears. Fainter, the rain outside — slowing now from earlier. The deep breaths of my husband, quickening, as his excitement built running his hands down my body. The scent of the room, smoky and old, musty bedding.

I climbed onto Magnus, straddled him, and tucked my nose against his neck breathing his scent in deep. It was thicker here, unwashed, but still gathering the scents around him — smoke and candle wax and even still the lingering scent of our shampoo from home and the oils I rubbed into his back before we left. I licked and nibbled his neck and met his lips with a deep kiss.

I shivered, Magnus pulled the blankets higher on my shoulders and tucked it around my legs. I sat up and used my fingers to trace his form under me. He was rubbing all over me. It felt delicious, blinded. As his excitement built mine did too and all the hate and anger of earlier in the day fell away.

It was just me loved by him, melting under his touch, shivering in the cold air, yet searing in the dips and valleys where we met. I folded over him, an elbow on each side of his face. He rubbed down my waist to my thighs, cupped my ass and brought me up and firmly down on him. His breath was a moan against my shoulder. His hands rubbed my breasts and moved down my hips massaging me up and down. I rose up to sitting and arched back, sensitive to every ridge of his prints on my skin. "You are so beautiful,"

I whispered, "You can't see me."

"I see ye. Glowing above me, solasta, my North Star, mo reul-iuil."

I breathed in his words with a deep warmth that flowed through my veins. I breathed out the words, "I love you, Magnus Campbell."

"Aye." He picked me up and brought me down and rubbed his hands around again, a rhythmic pattern — rub me up and then massage me down — mesmerizing me with the movements as intensity built. Long after I had forgotten that we had been talking, he said, "Tis the same for me, yet tis a brutal love, mo reul-iuil. I am afraid of ye. Afraid for ye." His voice vibrated in his chest, under my palms as I rode his waves. He pulled me up and pushed me back. "I am weakened and wanting and if I try tae be strong and bold your touch brings me back to my knees."

My breath was quick and shallow, my thoughts spinning. Drips along my lips, I kissed him, rising and falling and touching and riding, "God, Magnus, oh my god. . . " having lost my ability to speak just — him, me, the infinite universe and —

He held my breasts raising and lowering me, meeting me on the ups and downs. Then he stilled, expectant, while I, with breaths that were like moans, continued to ride, faster and faster, until I burst apart, losing myself with a sound like a wail. I finished — spent. He kissed my neck and brought me up and down taking another long moment before, with his own moan, he finished too.

His arms went around my back and hugged me to his chest.

I kissed his cheeks, the ridge of his nose, tasted the salty sweat on his upper lips. "I'm a brutal love?"

"I dinna ken if ye were listenin'."

"Maybe not with my ears. It was hard to listen while you

were rocking me like that, but in my heart I heard every word. I want to make you happy — don't I make you happy?"

"'Tis a conflict, that ye are my love and my happiness and my pleasure." He pressed his hips against me. He was now soft and insignificant, but the moment before had been so spectacular that my breath quickened at the memory of it. "Yet I am furious ye are so powerful. I may nae survive ye."

"Magnus, you may break my heart again talking like this."

His voice whispered in my ear. "I know, mo reul-iuil. I know. But tis a truth I must warn ye of. I love ye, and tis brutal that ye are alive three hundred years away. I am borrowing ye against time." He kissed up my neck and across my cheek to my lips.

"I'm right here, on you, flesh and blood. I am yours and time and space don't matter. We transcend. That is the truth of it." I pulled my hips up and away and slid to his side, tucked under his arm, draped across his chest.

"Aye, but when ye hated me today, twas the darkest moment of my life."

In his voice I could hear the pauses growing, the rhythm slowing, the rumble deepening, as he slid toward sleep.

"And you've been whipped."

"Aye, I have been whipped. But when ye hated me twas worse."

"I could never really hate you. Those were just words. I'll be more careful with them in the future."

"Me as well, mo reul-iuil." And then he slowly relaxed and the dark enveloped us as first he fell asleep and then I. . .

$\mathcal{I}$ woke to a bone-chilling cold. Far worse than in the middle of the night. Dawn was the coldest I had ever been. I could see my breath while we were under the blankets. Magnus built a fire, yet still I had to leave the bed to get near it. And yes, my lip balm lid was chewed and the stick of it gone. That rat was a total jerk.

While I dressed and then Magnus tightened the laces on my back, he went over what we needed to accomplish. He said, "You need tae ask Lady Mairead where Lord Delapointe is keeping his vessel. It must be there in the castle. Also ask her where the third vessel is. She must have hidden it somewhere. Then you need tae—"

"I need to make a list. I suppose paper and pencil would be too much trouble? Wait, I have my phone. But I don't want to run down the battery."

"In case ye need tae make a call?" We both laughed.

"I hate phone lists anyways, I can't cross through the entries."

He continued. "If he winna let ye see her, I need tae know if

Lady Mairead is imprisoned. If so, try to determine where in the castle she is being kept. Perhaps we can plan an escape..."

I turned and he pushed up my breasts as he tightened the cord on the front. "You're getting good at this."

"I greatly prefer the undressing, but your cleavage is a hint of what is under there. Tis verra nice."

"You're a scoundrel."

"You're my wife. I consider myself lucky I find ye so attractive. Could be far worse. You could have the face of a pig." He leaned down and kissed me on the top of my jiggling cleavage.

"That is not my face, sir Magnus."

He grinned and then returned to the list. "If you have the chance tae get Delapointe's vessel, get your hands on it and journey home. I will be right behind ye. If you canna get tae the vessel, run out of the castle, I will be waitin'. And we both go back together with the one I have in my sporran."

I nodded. It all made sense, complicated, but reasonable. Except the part where I left without him, but what were the odds I'd have Lord Delapointe's vessel, anyway?

He added, "Come out by nine at night."

"Okay, easy."

He held my waist and looked in my eyes. "Not easy. Hard. Lady Mairead is nae tae be trusted, but her brother, the Earl? He is trustworthy, yet verra slippery. He is always playin' a game, always strategizin'. He loves a battlefield. He will play us all like soldiers without worryin' a bit about our lives. And for sport he likes to pit people against each other. If he is helpin' us, tis because he wants somethin' in return."

"It couldn't just be that he wants to not look weak? Lord Delapointe Is holding his sister and held his nephew. It serves him to look strong to demand knowledge of their whereabouts."

"True, but watch him. There will be ulterior motives. If

anything happens in the walls of the castle I will climb them tae get tae ye." He handed me a knife.

"Is this yours?"

He nodded and gestured for me to raise my skirts. He strapped the knife just below my knee. Then he used soot from the hearth to scuff all over the tops of my too rubber, too new, too-foreign sneakers.

We stood still and looked at each other. "I know ye have agreed Kaitlyn, but I have tae ask again — please, go. If you have a vessel in your hands, go."

"What if you need me? I have those mad fighting skills."

He half-smiled. "I know ye are being funny. I am good at fighting though, remember I can handle myself. I can." He pulled my chin up and looked me in the eyes. "You daena need tae save me. Save yourself. Please."

I nodded.

"Do ye promise?"

"I promise."

He kissed me sweetly.

We descended to the great hall to get some thick and crusty, rock-hard bread for breakfast. I wished desperately for some coffee, but wishes don't work with the impossible.

We went to the stables. It was very, very ice cold outside. I was wrapped in two wool shawls, but my feet were ice cubes. We each got a horse. Problem was, I was afraid to ride by myself. And my horse reared unhappily, menacingly, whenever I tried to get near it.

Magnus would ride with me on his horse. We would lead mine.

We waited on the path, seated on Magnus's horse, for his Uncle and his six men to join us. But after a short while only two men appeared over the hill. Magnus grunted. "Tis only Sean and Ewan."

He turned our horse to meet them.

Ewan's face was blackened blue, swollen, and scabbed. He wore an angry scowl. Thankfully, he kept his eyes averted from my face. Sean, big and burly and gregarious, spoke in Gaelic at great speed about something while Magnus's face drew serious.

He explained to me, "The Earl canna attend ye tae the castle. He has been called away because of an uprising and canna afford tae spare the extra men. I am again with two. You have only two men tae go tae the castle with ye. And one of them is Ewan. I told the Earl I winna stand for him being in your company, but he has either forgotten or daena care."

Sean spoke in English for my benefit. "It will be good Mags. Look at me, the Earl has made sure ye have the best men. We will take care of Kaitlyn for ye."

Magnus scowled. "Sean — if anythin' happens."

"What could happen, Mags? Ewan is the favored nephew of the Earl of Breadalbane. You are my brother. We will protect your wife as our own."

Magnus agreed, apprehensively. Ewan and Sean mounted horses and we all headed east toward Talsworth castle.

At first the dirt road was wide and flat and accommodating. Magnus and I rode beside Sean, and the two brothers talked and laughed a lot. Ewan rode behind, quiet and sullen. Then as time passed, the road became smaller, increasingly rutted, and more difficult to traverse. We rode in single file: Sean, then Ewan, then me and Magnus riding behind. We lost them occasionally and caught up. Or rode faster, passed them, and waited for them to catch up. The conversations between Sean and Magnus were hilarious. They told long stories, unbelievable stories, about adventures that would surely have killed them if the stories had been true.

Ewan was surly, but no one seemed concerned about it, as if it was simply his personality, and not the behavior of a rapist monster who should be in jail. I was very bitter and hated him a lot.

Occasionally we passed farms. The road broadened. The fields looked much like fields from my time. For a while the road turned around a loch. The air was colder. The wind blustered, but when we entered woods the air warmed a bit. Magnus said, "We are only an hour away now." I wondered how he knew his way.

We had a moment alone and Magnus said, "I have been wantin' tae ask ye somethin'."

"That sounds serious."

"Tis. I canna get it off my mind."

I steeled myself for a big important something. "Okay, ask."

"The other night, Chef Zach made Buffalo Wings. I have been thinking on them since. I saw a buffalo hide while I was in London once and canna figure about the wings."

Luckily my head was turned so he couldn't see my stifled laughter. "They're actually chicken wings. The recipe came from a city, Buffalo, New York."

"Ah. So the buffalo dinna have wings, makes more sense."

"When we get home, I'll take you to the Jacksonville Zoo, show you all the animals. But you saw a hide?"

"Och aye, a hide and some other treasures from the new world. They were on display at court."

"Last night you told the Earl that you hadn't been at court."

"I haena discovered what side he will end up on. At times he has been on the side of the monarchy, but now that King William has passed I dinna ken he will be a Jacobite. If he thinks I have been a friend of the monarchy, he may well think my side has been decided. Tis dangerous tae have my side decided by someone else."

"It sounds really complicated. I kind of wished I had paid

attention in my history classes. Though this is British history, American history is different."

"Och aye, perchance when we get home we ought tae do some learnin' on it, see what side I ended on."

"The past tense in that sentence kind of freaks me out."

"I am the past. Tis nae sensible tae deny the truth."

"I guess since I'm here, I'm the past too. Oh man, what if I looked myself up, and I'm in the history books? That's super freaky."

"I canna bear the thought of ye ending here, mo reul-iuil. Let us please talk of other things."

"Okay, buffalo wings then, that's really what you've been thinking about?"

"And ice cream and pasta and—"

"Chocolate and coffee."

"Aye, coffee."

~

Finally we reached the end of the forest. At a low stone wall, beside a large oak tree, we all came to a halt.

Magnus said, "You will need tae ride alone now."

"Yeah, sure, okay."

Magnus dropped from his horse and I slid into his arms. Who was going to do this for me?

Magnus said, "I will wait here, until nine. If you arna returned I will come get ye. In the odd chance I find myself scaling walls, while ye find ye'self escapin', return tae this spot. I will leave ye a message here, just under this rock, see?" He pushed aside a bush that stood at the inside corner of the wall.

"Also, see this tree?" He pointed up at the branches.

"And then look back at the castle, see the line of the wall there, note the size?"

I said, "Worst case scenario. I'll get back here."

"And ye journey. Just go, I will follow."

I started to say no, but stopped. "Okay, worst case, I come here by myself and I journey home, by myself."

"Worst case," he agreed. He held my horse, talked calmly to it in Gaelic, and heaved me from behind up into the seat. Harder than before because I was wearing thirty pounds of wool clothing.

Sean joked, "Not much use for horse riding in the West Indies?"

Magnus adjusted a buckle. "Their horses are smaller and faster. They are called Mustangs. Kaitlyn is quite adept at driving them. But these speak Gaelic and are higher than she is used tae."

"Ah, perhaps our new relations could ship one tae me. I should like tae add it tae my stables."

Magnus helped me shove my foot into the stirrups, impossible to see under my skirt. I was definitely incompetent. Anyone could see. "I'll have my father send a Mustang along with the sugar for the Earl."

Next Magnus spoke to Ewan, his words loud, guttural, and angry. Ewan answered his words short and snarling. Sean aimed his horse between them, parting them, and pulled alongside me. He said something in Gaelic, short and clipped like a bark that caused Ewan to quiet with a scowl.

Magnus handed my reigns to Sean and patted me on the thigh. "I will be here when ye return. Be safe, mo reul-iuil."

I nodded and Sean, Ewan, and I turned and trotted out of the forest toward looming Talsworth leaving Magnus. He stood forlorn watching me go. He had my vessel, the only way to return to my century. And I was headed the opposite direction. I was terrified, no matter what I said yesterday. The last thing I wanted to do was live here eating rabbits.

CHAPTER 25

a wide road led up to the large castle, actually much more like a palace, sprawling, majestic. A light stone facade, it was double in scale of Balloch. With many windows, a real estate agent's dream. And I was way more frightened. Our horses kicked up a cloud of dust up a drive to the front. I held tight to the saddle because they were leading me far faster than I wanted to go. I listed to the side occasionally and tried desperately to hang on. Sean spoke with guards, settled on a place to tie our horses, and held out his arms for me to slide into.

This was a huge mistake. I knew I was a foreigner in a strange land, but I was also on a dangerous mission. I could barely speak the language and I had never seen any of this before. I took a deep breath and tried to get on top of my rising panic.

I concentrated on my guard, Sean and Ewan, both so big, hulking, broad-shouldered that I felt protected walking between them. Even though Ewan was a terrifying monster. At least it wasn't directed at me anymore, but that was barely a comfort. I seriously didn't know how I was dealing with him — this was such a scary situation I couldn't worry about the man that attempted to rape me yesterday? Though he was inches away?

I felt disconnected from myself, watching from the outside. Possibly the fear was causing a psychotic episode. Fuck, were there therapists here? My hands shook. My breath was ragged. I tried to be Hayley's voice of reason, *Who's going to go up there and be a badass? Me. Who's going to rescue Lady Mairead, steal a time-traveling vessel, escape, and reunite with her husband in the woods in. . .* I couldn't continue because it was such total bullshit.

We were halfway up the wide steps to the imposing door, when from it stepped a man — dressed like out of an antique painting that would be titled 'Our Forefathers', powdered hair, breeches and a fitted coat, older, handsome, a broad smile across his face as if he expected us. Did he know we were coming?

"Welcome! Is this a surprise? I see there, Sean Campbell, son of my fair wife. Are thee well Sean? To what do I owe this pleasure?" He was British, so at least he was easier to understand.

Though his face smiled, it didn't rise to his eyes.

From above me on the stairs he sized me up and down, took in the look of Ewan's bludgeoned face, appraised Sean, and settled back on me with a questioning look.

Sean said, "Lord Delapointe, I have the honor of presenting my newly arriv'd sister, Kaitlyn Campbell, wife of Magnus Campbell, we are—"

"Kaitlyn Campbell! Well, well, a daughter!" He magnanimously swept down the steps and clasped my hands in both of his. "I am thrilled. And what a beauty." He swept my hands out and appraised me awkwardly. I blushed and looked away. I was in way over my head. I glanced at Sean who interrupted, "Madame Campbell is here tae speak with Lady Mairead."

He arched his brow, "Ah! Well, Mairead has just been taken to bed with an ill-defined ache and plans to stay there until the morrow. But when she hears of your arrival, Kaitlyn, I am sure she will rally. Please, come in, come in. But not all of you, just Kaitlyn. We don't want to over-press Mairead's health."

Sean's brow furrowed, "Nae, I am tae attend Madame Campbell into the castle. I have some messages for Lady Mairead as well. The Earl has asked me tae give them tae her directly." Sean leveled his gaze and stood firm.

"Ah, yes yes," said Lord Delapointe. "Fine, as a son of Mairead, you are always welcome." Then he added, "And you Ewan, I do love to hear a battle tale and your face has a history about it. Come." Sean and Ewan exchanged a glance. Sean lightly held my elbow guiding me up the stairs following Lord Delapointe into the interior halls.

I whispered to Sean, "Have you been here before?"

Lord Delapointe interjected, "The Campbell clan has refused us the honor of their visits until now. Lady Mairead feels the slight quite acutely, I assure you."

I glanced behind me, Ewan was scanning left and right as we followed the passageways. The interior rooms we passed through were best described as opulent.

I asked, "Will you send a message to Lady Mairead that I'm here? My business is urgent."

"Certainly." He brought us to two guards standing in front of large closed doors. The guards opened the doors for him with a bow. The room we entered was amazing, lush and expensive-looking, with sweeping ceilings, gorgeous art, marble sculptures, ornate furniture, and exquisite rugs. I forced myself not to gape.

A small sitting area, a few chairs, a couch, and small tables were set at one end of the room near the fire. He offered us seats. "This is my cabinet. I hope you don't mind. My public rooms are too large for the type of conversation we will be having."

The two guards followed us into the room and now stood guarding the inside.

Lord Delapointe settled himself into a chair, sitting back

comfortably. He had loads of charm, and a smile that looked overly practiced. His cold eyes chilled me all the way through.

I sat on the small settee to his left, Sean sat on the chair to my left. Ewan stood behind Sean facing the fire.

"Will your cousin not sit?"

"My cousin is more comfortable outdoors than in, always has been."

"Fine fine," said Lord Delapointe. His eyes studied the side of Ewan's ravaged face.

There was literally so much going on here, I felt sure someone more adept, Lady Mairead for instance, or Oprah, would be able to figure out the nuances of the conversation. But the tiny pauses were beyond me. It felt very, very dangerous.

Sean and Ewan wouldn't have come though unless they thought it was safe. Sean's expression remained at ease so I was probably overreacting. Yet the guards were literally in the room with us.

"I really need to speak to Lady Mairead, please. Will you tell her I'm here?"

He leaned back languidly with a malevolent smile. "Where is your accent from? I'm having trouble placing it?"

"I grew up in the West Indies."

"And where did you meet my stepson, Magnus?"

"In London, about three months ago, we wed soon after."

"Ah, see, this is wonderful. Magnus was here, not long ago, visiting his mother, and he did not mention it. Tis a pity. I would have celebrated with him. And where is he now?" His voice had gone vague and disinterested, as if he really wanted to know, but was keeping his voice measured so as not to let me know how very much he wanted to know.

He was a super-villain and I was very much hoping for Batman to appear.

Or Magnus.

But this was a very dangerous place for Magnus. Heck, it was dangerous for me. I just hadn't realized it until I heard the slithery voice of my step-father-in-law.

"That's why I'm here, I haven't seen him since just after our wedding. I was hoping Lady Mairead would know how to find him." I added, "The Earl is worried about him."

"Ah, his uncle. Yes. The Earl is worried about his nephew. Why didn't he attend his niece on this visit? Oh, that's right, the uprisings. He's on the right side, the Earl, at least, though his methods are not quite as thorough as I would have wanted."

He stood and walked to the back of his chair. "I'll go and tell Lady Mairead you're here. See if she will accompany us at dinner. Make yourself at home." He swept from the room.

Sean said, "We canna stay for dinner—" He glanced at the door, the guards were still stationed there.

"I have to see Lady Mairead before we go."

Sean nodded. "Dost ye agree Ewan?"

"Aye."

"Okay, we wait for dinner. Hopefully tis good, I'm famish'd." And just like that the two men went completely blank, staring into space. Me, on the other hand. — I was about to fidget out of the room with nerves. I wanted to go on Facebook or Instagram. Scroll through my friends' pages, look at their photos. Hayley, Zach, Emma, even Michael took cool photos. Quentin's were weird; he liked guns, cars.

I opened my bag and glanced down in it. I had a wallet with some IDs and credit cards, my phone, keys, some Midol, and tampons stuffed in the side pocket. I would probably start my period day after tomorrow, great. Hopefully not in the 1700s where underpants were nonexistent. I clicked the bag closed again with a sigh. There was literally nothing in there that would help. I tried to go as blank as Sean and Ewan.

Finally, after more than an hour, Lord Delapointe breezed

back in. "Mairead is just thrilled you're here. She's promised to do her best to come to dinner. We'll leave her a place." He offered me an arm to escort me out of the room and through the castle to his great hall. He stopped along the way to show me tapestries, sculptures, and paintings of note. I paused dutifully and admired, but my heart and mind weren't in it. I was too creeped out by holding his arm to be able to concentrate.

I had now been in two castles. One felt like what my mother would have called 'old money,' a phrase used to be complimentary. And one felt like 'new money,' a term used to be insulting. Lord Delapointe's Talsworth Castle was ostentatious, overly done, and too lavish. Balloch castle had been cold and fortress-like, simpler, yet felt important and historic. I supposed it was all very historic from my point of reference. How many times had I said something was from 'the Middle Ages'? I had often put a good portion of the past into that one time period, the twelfth century, fifteenth, eighteenth, it had never dawned on me that I should care what happened when. I never thought it would be applicable. It was all just a lot of very, very old.

Except for the long dimensions and sweeping ceiling, Lord Delapointe's dining room was the complete opposite of the Earl's. A long table, but covered with a table cloth. Thirty or more chairs only six places set. Five at one end and at the long, far away other end of the table, one setting. The table settings looked expensive — glassware, silverware, and china. Lord Delapointe had me sit at his left. Sean beside me. Scanning the room as we took our seats. Ewan sat across from me and Lord Delapointe sat at the head of the table, quite fussily I might add, "Well, isn't this exquisite? A family dinner." He looked down the table at the conspicuously empty chair with the full dinner setting in front of it and I knew with certainty that Lady Mairead would not be joining us. Was she imprisoned or just gone?

Ewan was flanked by two of Lord Delapointe's men. Sean and Ewan exchanged a look and a small nod.

We exchanged niceties while we waited for our food. Sean ordered beers from a server and passed them to me and Ewan. He seemed at ease, but always scanning the room. I wished I could get him to just call off the meal, stand up, and take me away. But a pit of dread had settled in my stomach.

It was too late to leave—

Lord Delapointe leaned in and said, "So what happened to your pretty face?"

I was confused for a second. My hand went to my face but Lord Delapointe's hand got there first. He stroked the back of his finger down my cheek. The sore one, the one with the bruise.

He was touching me and it was way past appropriate the way he lingered. And there was literally nothing I could do.

"Nothing, just ran into something. Clumsy."

"The Earl has sent my daughter to me injured. He might be more careful." His hand rubbed down my face again. Okay, back home there would be some serious pepper-spraying on this perv. Where the hell was my pepper spray?

I glanced at Ewan to see what he was thinking about the bruise and the discussing of it, because sadly, though he was a total monster and caused the injury, he was right now one of my only two protectors. His eyes met mine.

Lord Delapointe flicked his eyes back and forth between me and Ewan and then I saw within his eyes a moment of recognition. "Ah, I see. My daughter has been bruised and battered in the house of Campbell and this is the violator sitting here at my dinner table." He leveled his gaze on Ewan.

Ewan growled. "Tis none of your business. Take your hands off her face."

"Because you're the favorite nephew of the Earl of Breadalbane, the only price you pay is a bruising? Then you are allowed to be her bodyguard?"

I said, "That's not really what happened."

"Not really," he said. He spun his pewter beer mug around and around. He slowly looked up — piercing eyes, mischievous glint. "Who bruised your face Ewan?"

Ewan looked across the table at Sean then answered. "I daena have tae answer your questions."

"True, but there's a young woman, my stepdaughter, a guest in my castle with a bruise upon her face and there you sit, a criminal..."

The two guards stepped up behind Ewan and struggled him up from the chair. He fought, yelling in Gaelic, twisting in their arms. Sean raced around the table, his knife drawn, battling two more guards. While Ewan kicked his chair back trying to get an arm free to draw a weapon.

I was yanked from my seat. Lord Delapointe had me by the arm, twisting it, pulling me to a back door.

I dragged my feet and pulled against him, writhing and screaming and begging—

One of the guards pulled a knife and slit Ewan's throat from one side to the other. His head lolled forward. Blood rushed down his clothes. He was shoved brusquely to the dirt floor, a sack of lifeless human. Once a monster, now my next-to-last hope, gone.

Sean looked down at his dead cousin and then turned to see me — pulled through a door to the dark, dangerous, alone parts of the castle.

The last look between us, nothing. Nothing helpful at all. Sean was wrestled to the ground, and I had no idea whether he was dead or alive.

Lord Delapointe's hands were clammy on my wrists. My arms were twisted and my body was forcibly moved. My mind was too shocked to be able to formulate an idea. I stubbed a toe on a step and then another as I was dragged up a stairwell of uneven stone. It was dark, very dark.

Lord Delapointe shoved me through a door into a hall. Was I on the third floor? What would I do, yell for help from a window? Would Magnus climb up here by himself?

I was in freaking Hogwarts, and I didn't have a magic wand.

I was dragged, shoved, and wrestled for so far and so long that I had no idea where I was. Up or down, east or west. I had forgotten to concentrate on where I was, and I was lost. I would need a bread trail to figure out how to get to a main door. If there was ever any chance of escape.

I had nothing left to lose, so I went for outrage. "I demand to see Lady Mairead. You have killed one of my family members, one of your wife's nephews. You will answer for this."

He shoved me through a door and there I was again, in his private cabinet. I stood still in the middle.

"Have a seat."

The room had grown dark, gloomy, cold. I could barely see a foot away. I continued to stand, but I was shaking, freezing, and worried I might fall. He lit a candle and placed it on the small table beside a chair near the fire. I couldn't resist; I dropped into the seat. Fine, but I wouldn't be comfortable. I kept my back straight, my hands clasped in my lap. My eyes directly ahead.

The flame of the candle cast a small pool of flickering light about six inches around. It wasn't enough. Lord Delapointe sat in a chair close to mine and if he leaned forward, the light illumi-nated his malevolent face. But when he leaned back, outside of the pool of light, his expressions and movements were hidden. It was terrifying like I was blind in pieces.

"I want to return to Sean Campbell. He has been ordered not to leave me and you have no jurisdiction over—"

Lord Delapointe stepped across the space, out of my field of vision. I heard him crouch down to stoke the fire. "Who has ordered him?" His back was to me. I had a knife. I could just stab him. I would hike my skirt, undo the knife — he turned with a long metal stick, red hot at the end. "Who has beaten the man, Ewan?"

"The Earl punished him. I don't know why you're asking this..."

"Magnus Campbell, you mean. Magnus Campbell, who is now waiting for word of you at the edge of my forest—"

My breath caught.

"—or *was*." His smile widened. "Right now he is being apprehended by my men." He admired the end of the poker. His face loomed into my light, glowing with the red of the heated stick. "It's been a good day for me. I didn't seek a fight, yet I have somehow conquered some of the best warriors of the Campbell clan."

My anger boiled over. I said, "Jesus Christ, do you have to sound like such a sick fuck?"

His brow went up. He lost his step for a moment. "Pardon?"

"Where I come from there's an archetype, a god-dammed stereotype — it's called super villain and really you're such a fucking cliche — have you been reading comic books?"

My hands trembled, I tried to keep them still over my anger, but I was growing wild.

"Comic books?"

My eyes glanced to the window — not really any moon at all, a faint glow. Would it be possible to jump from here? If this dickhead wasn't here, knocked out or something, could I bust out the glass, squeeze through, and jump? How many floors up were we?

"Yes, comic, comedy, joke books. You're like a character from one, with your tiny little mind and your jackass, malevolent smile."

I was pretty sure this was the third floor. Plus, the landing would probably be onto solid, body-breaking, brick pavers.

I continued, "Is that the kind of jerk-ass smile you had plastered across your face while you beat Magnus?"

His smile turned slithery, exactly what I was talking about. "You know more than you have admitted. Your husband was my guest not three weeks ago. He disappeared from my jail."

"Well, I don't know anything about that, but I'm so glad he escaped from your twisted little prison palace."

He quickly grabbed my face in a claw-like hand. Pressed close. His face not an inch away.

"You don't sound like how a girl raised by a gentle British family in the West Indies would sound."

I glared into his eyes. The red hot poker was just a few inches from my face. "It's the mother fucking New World asshole, no one is gentle there."

His breath was hot and gross on my face. He ignored me and closely inspected the bruise on my cheekbone.

I said, "You know, until just a few minutes ago Ewan Campbell was the biggest monster I knew. Congratulations, you've been crowned king supreme of the mega monsters."

He shoved my chin away, tossing me to the arm of my chair. He laughed loudly and menacingly.

I righted myself fast. I had to keep him in my sights; he was too unpredictable. He tossed the poker into the fire. I glanced toward the door trying to make out in the darkness if the guards were standing there. They could have moved closer for all I knew. Or left the room altogether.

Lord Delapointe brought me back to the conversation from his position crouched in front of my knees. "Mairead too is gone. I suppose you haven't seen her? I had something I needed to speak to her about."

My breath was coming ragged and hard. "Good, I'm glad she got away, I hope she's long gone."

He grinned widely, maniacally. "You have taught me a lot this visit daughter. You are a true gift."

"What the hell are you talking about?"

"I seem to have found myself in possession of a magical device. I have been attempting to understand its purposes and uses, yet every man who uses it returns dead or on the edge of death. I believed that the mere act of using it was what killed them. And then I supposed that perhaps they traveled to a brutal age and that is how they have died. But you have crossed from that time. You survived the jump and are unscarred and healthy. Your only blemish is from the brutes my wife calls family."

I grunted and crossed my arms. Pouting because I hadn't realized how much he was able to learn. "I don't know what the fuck you're talking about. I want Sean Campbell, my escort, brought to me directly. My father, John Sheffield, will have you in jail for the way I have been treated here today."

He paused, then icily said, "You are in no position to make demands my dear. That is not how this works." He stood, stepped out of the pool of light and through the darkness toward the door into complete blackness. I was terrified he might actually leave, and I wouldn't know if I was alone.

He spoke under his voice to someone near the door.

Then he said loudly to me, "Don't touch anything, or my guards have permission to move you to a cell." He banged out of the room, leaving me in pitch darkness, except for the tiny flickering candle beside my arm. A few feet away a small pile of coals smoldered in the hearth.

I looked down at my hands in the dark. Were the guards even here and were they inside the door or outside? How many were there, and where were they? It was very quiet, I couldn't determine. I said, "Hello?"

No sound.

I listened, on edge. Every nerve was stretched to listen. I was about to stand up, look around the room, but then I could hear it — faint breathing from the door. At least one man was inside with me. Could they see me? Probably. I was sitting in a pool of light.

I hoped there weren't rats in here with me.

Okay, also I was starving. I hadn't eaten anything downstairs and my shaking from anger had turned into a low blood sugar sort of near-faint tremble. That did not seem helpful. I shifted my purse to my lap, opened my bag, and looked inside — nothing. I did remember the painkillers in there, six. If I could get them into his food, then wait for an hour, he might be incapacitated enough. I could get away. But there were too many what ifs.

He hadn't taken my leg knife though.

But with my puny stab the knife would easily glance off his wool coat unless I was standing over him. So maybe the painkillers first, then the knife? That would be a cold-hearted bitch move though. Was I capable of murdering someone?

Probably, if he smiled like that one more time.

He was gone for close to an hour. In all that time I didn't move — but my panic grew. My breaths rang in my ears. My heartbeat battered my chest.

He returned with a bang of the door and told the guards to leave us. A moment later he appeared in my field of vision and tossed a plate of food on the table beside me. "Eat."

He grabbed the other chair and pulled it directly in front of mine, almost knee to knee. It crossed my mind that there might be something in the food, much like I had just been plotting.

He watched my face noticing my hesitation. "My wife Mairead practiced the arts of poison, every headache I ever suffered could be traced to one of her foul moods. Keeping her locked in her chambers has been my only recourse."

"Is she still there?"

"That foul son of hers helped her escape months ago. I haven't seen her since." His eyes cut to me. "And since you haven't seen young Magnus. . . Mairead did not attend your wedding?"

"No."

"Well, that is unfortunate, she would have enjoyed meeting you. She greatly enjoys ritual sacrifice." He leaned back, comfortable, sociopathic, bone-chillingly scary.

"Eat and then we can discuss the deal you will make with me."

I brought the plate to my lap and ate meat and carrots with my hands. He looked somewhat proud of the meal he was providing, so I mentioned it was bland to provoke him. With the food energizing me I regained even more of my insolence.

He said, "Pass over your bag," and wiggled his fingers expectantly.

I looped it off my shoulder and passed it to him. He pulled out the contents: the bottle of painkillers, the antibiotics, the bandaids. He turned a tampon over and over in his hand. What a dumbass. He inspected my car keys, one that was electronic, three house keys. Then my phone. He flipped it over and over in his hand while I ate.

"What is this?"

"A magical box."

"What does this one do?"

I took it from him and pushed the home button. I showed him the home screen with the apps. He pushed at it tentatively and kept turning it over to check the other side. That was cute as hell when Magnus was doing it, but down right irritating to watch this evil man try it. Clearly he was an idiot.

I was way smarter. I just had to think my way out of this situation. "I want my stuff back."

He ignored me, opened my wallet, and pulled out a small stack of credit cards, gift cards, and my license. What if I left one of those behind and three hundred years from now someone found my photo ID in the ruins of this castle?

He leaned to the light and investigated my license, but seemed not to know how to read the information on it.

I pushed the plate to the table — done eating and ready to get on with it. "You mentioned a deal? You should get to it; the Earl probably has an army headed here right now."

"Ah, but see, that's not exactly how it works here. It's much slower. Tell me about where you're from. What did you call it, the West Indies? They have interesting shoes."

I glanced down. My feet, the sneakers, were sticking out from my dress. "I'm not telling you anything until I know that Sean Campbell, my escort, is okay. You sack of—"

He pulled from behind his chair a sporran. The straps were cut short. He banged it to the floor between us. "Formerly belonging to the young Magnus."

My eyes went wide, and he chuckled. "My prisons are full of the clan Campbell. Leave it to Mairead to disappear right when we are entertaining her family."

"Is he alive?"

"For now. He will stay that way if you cooperate."

"Fine, what do you want?"

"I am in line to the British crown — have you heard this, Kaitlyn?"

"Nope, only that you are a total dick. Can't imagine you'd be a good choice for a ruler."

"It's not a matter of choice, but of bloodline. I'm not very close, but close enough, and if bloodline doesn't suffice, and sometimes during upheaval and confusion, bloodline isn't enough. . ." He lazily rolled his hand as if to infer that something would need to be done. "I thought marrying a Campbell would give me an army at my disposal, but my brother-in-laws are too busy with their own orchestrations to help me with mine. So that leaves the dowry of Mairead. Married before, as you know, to a foreigner with magical gifts. She has given me one and with a little persuasion she has given me the directions for using it."

"I saw the cuts you made to her face."

"She was irresolute until then. She chose the price she would pay for not sharing her wealth with her husband."

"God, you are such an ass. How did you get her to marry you?"

"I took her. Such as one does here in Scotland. How did your Scot win you?"

I did not want to say 'by contract.' Instead I refocused. "You know, I need to look in the sporran."

"Ah, of course, my stepdaughter doesn't trust me."

I snatched it up and looked inside. Empty. Completely empty. Was this Magnus's? It was fur and I hadn't really...it looked a lot like it, but...

"You doubt my word Kaitlyn?"

"I do. Magnus killed your brother. He escaped you once already, I think if you found him, he'd be dead right now. So either you have Magnus, or he's dead. If he's alive, I'll need proof."

He shook his head slowly. I could barely make out his movements in the dimness. But then he hunched toward me, his face jutting into the light. "See, again, you think you're the one making deals. I have one of the machines, I can travel to the future and the past. I need you for nothing except courtesies, dear daughter Kaitlyn, and if you don't help — well, you can die with your husband. It's nothing to me. As a matter of fact, it helps my case to have you all die on your visit here. Sends a clear message to the Earl — I will not be disregarded." He punctuated the last words with his finger on the arm of the chair.

I gulped and took an edifying breath. "What do you want?"

One of my warriors has returned from your time wounded. He told me of wondrous weapons, amazing accuracy, and very deadly. I would like an arsenal of these new weapons, and I would like your help getting them. In exchange I'll let some people live."

"Why don't you go get them? I don't see what I have to do with it."

"You can guide me. Show me around, introduce me to the right people."

I heard yelling down the hall. Loud. Closer. Through the dark. And then, without a doubt, Magnus. He had been caught, or worse — turned himself in to get to me.

I chewed my lip.

Lord Delapointe watched my face.

A moment later a bang as the door flung open, voices in the room. Magnus struggling. He was dragged to the middle of the room, faint and shadowy in the darkness. I could barely see him. He was shoved to a kneeling position, nearer the light — his head yanked back. His eyes were black and swollen. His neck bulged with the want of beating the shit out of someone. Darkness dripped from a head wound, dark stains covered his shirt. His hands were bound in front.

"Kait—" A guard punched him on the side of the head and yanked him still.

I attempted to stand. "Magnus, they found you?" Lord Delapointe grabbed me by the wrist and forced me back to my chair.

"I came when ye dinna return, I came tae—"

"He killed Ewan. Oh my god, Magnus, it was awful—"

Lord Delapointe said, "Ah, isn't this wonderful, a reunion? Yes, yes, Magnus, you'll be glad to hear your cousin paid for the harm he caused Kaitlyn. I'm certain you will be thankful."

Magnus spit on the floor.

The two guards yanked him erect. His neck muscles pressed outward, his body trembled with rage. I thought for a moment he might go Incredible Hulk and bust through his ropes, but he couldn't; he was a man not a superhero. And this was an overwhelming mess.

Lord Delapointe said "Tell your husband about the deal we just made."

I wasn't fully aware we had agreed to anything, but I had gotten the gist. "I'm going to travel to the future with him—"

"Nae Kaitlyn."

"And I'm going to help him get some weapons to bring back. He has promised he'll release you when we return—"

"Kaitlyn, tis a dangerous idea. Ye canna—"

"I'll do this one thing, and then we can be together."

Lord Delapointe said, "Good, so we are all agreed."

Magnus said, "I am nae agreed. Kaitlyn, I told ye I could handle this. Daena make any deals."

Lord Delapointe walked around the back of my chair and disappeared in the darkness. He reappeared behind me, barely illuminated, near the window looking out over the square below.

Magnus, gestured with his hands for me to come to the space right in front of him. He mouthed, "Come here."

I took a deep breath. "Lord Delapointe, he has blood dripping down his face. Please let me clean his wound. I have a bandage in my bag."

I could hear what sounded like a drawer opening and paper rustling. He said, "No."

"You have assured me you are not a brutal man, that you are dignified, even royal. It's no secret I believe you're a complete and total sack-of-shit ass-clown, but this is your chance to prove me wrong. We have a deal. I'm asking as your step-daughter to give me the chance to put a bandage on my husband's face before I go away."

Papers flicked, a book slammed. "Fine, fine."

The two hulking guards flanked Magnus, keeping him under control.

I went to the small side table and sifted through my bag's contents grabbing a couple of things: a bandaid, the antibiotic cream. I went to my husband, stood before him, and looked down. "Hello Love."

Blood dripped down his upturned face. One eye was swollen closed from the ass-kicking he just received.

"Mo reul-iuil, tis a fine mess we art in."

"Yes, he's a real dipstick so there's that. Maybe the biggest one I've ever known. Probably in history."

Magnus chuckled.

I tilted his face and pressed close to his front to steady him, me. "You have a gaping wound here Magnus, your face is not going to be as pretty."

I pulled up the front of my skirts and wiped the edges of his wound and then squeezed a bit of ointment on my finger.

I smeared it realizing that literally everything I was doing was full on filthy, but what choice did I have? I had to hope the ointment was stronger than the bacteria.

And it wasn't really about the bandaid at all —

It was about the broad cold steel of my knife as it slid past my calf. Magnus's bound hands pulling it free from the sheath he had attached there hours before.

My hands shook as I peeled the paper off the bandaid, spread it out, and pressed it to his skin.

He hid his hands holding the knife in the folds of my skirt. "Tis nae horseshit."

"Tis nae." I agreed.

Lord Delapointe asked, "What's that?"

Magnus growled, "Before you take my wife and possibly my life, I intend tae tell her I love her." He looked up at me,

"Strong as an oak, near a stone wall, aligned with a castle tower."

I nodded that I understood. I kissed his forehead as Lord Delapointe said, "Well, enough of that, we have a trip to make daughter."

Magnus said, "I will see ye on the other side."

I smiled at him, a sad smile, full of not knowing, and fear, and what-if-this-doesn't-work, but it had to, because this was it.

I stepped away to the side table that held my purse. I scooped the cards and wallet inside, slung it over my shoulder, and kept the keys in my fist.

Because I had learned a valuable lesson in college — one of the best of them all. That if it's late at night and you have a murderous monster rapist-creep following you, or harassing you, or scaring the ever-loving shit out of you, put a key between each finger. Poking out of your knuckles they make the closest thing you might have to an excellent weapon.

And what I needed right now was an excellent weapon.

CHAPTER 26

*L*ord Delapointe snarled to his guards. "You can take him to his cell now."

And I knew it was time for me to act. I walked through the darkness toward where I had last heard Lord Delapointe's voice and following my training, which had been to: One, swing first, using surprise as your element. And two, swing from low, near your hip, stepping forward to give your weak girl-arms momentum. And three, *do it, Kaitlyn, do it, just do it already, Magnus is going to* — I stepped forward and swung hard, up, fast, with all my strength, aiming right for the soft part on the neck just under Lord Delapointe's chin.

I wished there might be a giant, cartoon, Kapow! noise, but no, my fist glanced off his jaw knocking him off guard but without much more damage than a scrape. But as he twisted toward me, outraged, yelling, I frantically swept my hands over the table beside us. I could barely see at all, but there was something, a thick, metal, what was it? A metal tower, pole, thing. I raised it over my shoulder like a softball bat and swung, hard, aiming for his head and producing an epic and disgusting sound — Thunk!

Not as satisfying as a 'kapow,' but equally effective. He stumbled and fell to his knees grasping for my skirts.

I spun around — Magnus was in full battle with a guard with swords.

He yelled, "Run, Kaitlyn!"

I ran, stumbling over a fallen, probably dead, totally lifeless guard on my way to the door. Seeing nothing around me but black darkness. Hearing the yells and bellows and bloody curses of my husband fighting behind me.

I slammed through the door into a hall that was so fucking pitch black I wondered if I might have died back there. I glanced behind me. The room glowed compared to where I was now — complete and total blackness.

I put my hands out and rushed in the direction I believed we had come from earlier. I felt my way along walls, careful to watch my step on the uneven stone floor. Behind me, in the room down the hall, the fighting raged.

I found a small recessed area and pressed into it. I pawed through my bag for my iPhone, and turned on my flashlight. I peeked out of the recess, shining the light up and down the hall. I was still totally alone.

I swung the light about ten feet in front of me, checked my way, then hid it in my skirts while I ran a few steps. Then I checked again, repeating the process, check, rush, check, rush, until I found the top of stairs.

I raced down holding the wall. A few steps and I tripped, dropping my phone with a cracking sound — *shitshitshit* — the flashlight still worked — *thankyouthankyouthankyou*.

I reached the bottom floor and peered around the corner. It was another long hallway, torches lining the walls, but their light was shoddy and spotty. If I hustled from point to point, I could get to the doors at the end. But that was not where I wanted to go, the room beyond was well-lit.

I checked the opposite direction, darker — someone was coming.

Someone carrying a lantern along the passage.

I ducked into the stairwell and went as still as I could go. *Quiet, don't breathe, don't breathe, don't pass out.*

A woman passed, carrying a tray of food toward the lit room at the opposite end.

She must have come from the kitchen. The kitchen would probably be busy, but also, perhaps, easy enough to sneak through.

The corridor was clear. I ran the length of it to a door and passed through to another skinnier stair and followed it down to where it opened into a bustling room.

Perhaps eight women, though it looked like it could hold a lot more, were cleaning, wiping down, wrapping up from the night. It must have been late. Across the entire room was a door to the outside. Hidden in the doorway, I fumbled with my iPhone trying to turn off the flashlight pushing the goddam button over and over, offoffoffmotherfuckingbuttonoff. Finally it went out.

I held up my hands and stepped from my hiding place. "Excuse me, excuse me. Pardon me, excuse me." I hustled across the kitchen, holding my hands up, head-bowing, and excusing myself. "I'm sorry, excuse me, my apologies." All the women stood surprised and staring.

I made it to the door, backed, bowing out of it, into an icy blast of freezing air.

Then I bolted through a garden, scaled a small fence, shoved open another door that led through a thick wall, and then it was fields, fields, and more fields. I turned on my flashlight, and ran, shining the light a foot in front of me, thanking God, the universe, and my self-control, that I hadn't run down my iPhone's battery on something stupid. I ran. My heart racing, my body shivering, my ragged breaths barely escaping my throat. Until I made it to the tree line. I was going to disappear there, into the woods, at probably close to midnight in the 18th century, Scotland. This was an insane plan.

When I turned back to look where I had come from, the moon illuminated the stone edifice and — crap, I was not on the right side of the castle.

I held onto a tree, bent over, and tried to get my breath under control.

CHAPTER 27

*H*ow long would it take before soldiers came looking for me? Hours — or minutes? I would be easy to find, my freaking breathing was as loud as a Harley. I looked up at the castle and tried to figure out which direction I needed to go. It had been hours since I first looked at it, and there had been some extreme duress since then. Whatever I remembered about what it looked like — it didn't look like that *now*.

My guess was I was on the southeast corner. I needed to be on the middle of the west side. Maybe a mile away. Plenty of time for the soldiers to get there first and wait for me.

I needed to run.

The night was freezing. I didn't have enough clothes on at all. My breath was frosty, the ground wet and slippery. My sneakers didn't have enough traction, plus it had taken about three minutes before they were sopping wet. I scrambled over bracken and through bushes always keeping the fields to my right. I dove further into the forest when I had to go around fallen trees and boulders. But not too far in, because man, getting lost would suck.

Luckily there was a bit more ambient light now, but not enough. I clawed away branches and scrambled over rocks. Tripping over a tree trunk, I stumbled — and landed, spent, unable to go anymore.

I shone my light around, wondering if someone was watching the woods from the windows, or the walls. Would they see my light just in the woods, shining around? "I'm here, I'm here."

I had to run.

So I climbed to my feet and kept going.

The forest thickened. Over my shoulder the castle looked more like it had earlier that day. I held onto a tree and really looked — yes, it was the wall, just like Magnus had pointed out.

Left and right — no tree. But I was pretty close to finding it.

The castle was bigger than I remembered. I scrambled further into the woods, checking over my shoulder — still there — still there. I found a small clearing, big enough for three horses to stand. Over my shoulder the castle was in the perfect position.

I beamed the light around — there, twenty feet away, the tree — maybe?

I ran to it and stumbled over the stone wall. Not where I expected it to be, at all.

I held onto it, crouched, and felt along the rocks for the corner, forgetting my phone's light completely — now I could hear it: Yelling. Men's voices. Hooves galloping. Coming closer, calling, whistling, stamping — crap. I felt madly around.

The corner of the wall was right here, yes — corner, tree, tower. I dove over it and rustled through muddy soggy leaves and underneath something hard, warm, and smooth. My hands closed around it.

I recited the numbers as the horses galloped over the field, crashing through the underbrush, about to trample —

. . .

I was ripped from this world and flung screaming and writhing in pain to the next.

CHAPTER 28

I was back, technically. Trouble was I was in terrific pain and soaking wet, lying in about four inches of muddy water, tucked in vegetation, in what seemed like — I rose a bit and peered around. Yep, I was in a marsh.

I laid my head on my arm, keeping it out of the water just barely. Everything hurt. My lips. My eyelids. My toenails. I was ice cold. How long had I been jumping, minutes? It felt like hours. I might have frostbite. I couldn't feel anything, except everything was on fire. My hand was enclosed around something like a claw. It was the vessel. I shoved it into my purse floating in the water beside me.

Magnus had picked me up when he felt like this and carried me with men chasing him. What was I weak? Um yeah, but still, *getupgetupgetup*. I pulled on marsh grass to steady myself as I heaved to my feet. *What was that sound — oh yeah, me, screaming*. I shoved my hands over my mouth.

Alligators. Alligators were here, for sure. I scanned left and right. Closest shore was left. I somehow managed to drag myself, pulling against marsh grass, moaning. I struggled against the plough mud, squelching and squelching around and in my sneakers, grasping and pulling the hem of my heavy wool skirt. With the next step my foot splashed deep into a hole. I was in water to my chest. My skirt held me down, but there was no escaping the dress. The belt was below the water, the ties were in the back.

I pulled with all my strength against the drag of heavy gravity that was way way stronger than usual. "Aargh. Ugh. Agh—" There it went, my shoe, disappearing into the mud. I kept trudging, the word, *alligators*, driving me.

I didn't need my shoe. I was going to be okay. My house was just a couple of miles away. Because looming over my head was the lighthouse. I made it out of the marsh and fell face down in the grass with a cry, I was in the park where we played kickball. Egan's Creek. I was home, sort of.

I slept, a sleep of nightmares and fevers and agonies, and woke up freaking out on the bank of the marsh.

It was day, probably afternoon, though this whole thing, being alive in this much pain, was way confusing. My whole existence was a lot undecipherable.

I stumbled up the grassy slope, crossed the baseball diamond to the empty parking lot, and headed for the road out front. Four cars passed me, slowing down, staring. I must have been a frightful witch of a woman, crazy, haggard, bedraggled. I walked toward the beach, thinking, *if I could get there, I could walk down the beach home. For miles.*

I really needed a ride. Soon. Because — one shoe.

A myriad of other reasons.

And then Hayley's car pulled up beside me. She sat and stared. Her mouth opening and closing. Then her window slid down, "Kaitlyn, what the fuck, Kaitlyn? Oh my god, Kaitlyn is it you? Crap, girlfriend..." She drove the car to the side of the road, jumped out, and ran around the car. "Kaitlyn?"

"Yeah, hi. I've had a bit of a disaster." I reached for the car handle and yanked it open as she reached to open it too.

"Kaitlyn, you're back from rehab? This looks like, what happened to you?"

"What — rehab? What are you talking about?" I dropped into the seat and rested my head on the headrest. It felt good to be in a 2017 vehicle. It felt good to be sitting down. It felt good to have Hayley there. She would drive me home—

"Kaitlyn, *rehab*. You've been incommunicado for four months." She slammed my car door shut.

I stared at her as she walked around to her side of the car. As she sat down. As she started the car. "Hayley, what did you say?"

"I said, you've been gone for four months. We all thought you were coming back months ago, that must have been a huge problem, girlfriend. And you look terrible."

Where had I been — four months? What the— "I don't know how to... four months?"

"These don't look like rehab clothes. Are you in some kind of cult? Is that what's happening? Oh my god, did you escape?"

I closed my eyes. "No, not, but can you drive me home? I'm really cold and need to change into some warm clothes, and then maybe I can explain it. Four months?"

Hayley looked at the watch on her wrist. "I was meeting the boys at the Turtle. I'll take you to my house... let me call Michael first."

"I really want to go to my house. I need clothes, a shower, bed. And Magnus might show up there, anytime."

"Kaitlyn, you don't have a home anymore. You weren't coming back; no one knew where you were, and you didn't leave any instructions. Your parents closed it all down. It's gone. Look, let me call Michael. I'll take you to my house, and we'll talk this all out. Holy crap girl, I can *not* believe you're here, and dressed like that. Were you sleeping in the marsh?"

Before I could answer, she got Michael on the phone. "Hey babe, yeah, I just found Kaitlyn. . . I know, she's just back, suddenly, I can't believe it. . . She was just at the park on Sadler. . . I know and she's. . . look, let me take her to my place. I won't make it tonight... " She listened for a few moments then said to me, "Michael and James are coming to the house, they want to know what happened too."

I groaned.

She said into the phone, "She said, 'great.' Pick up beer. . . Thanks, see you in a bit."

She tossed the phone to the console between our seats. "What the hell? I have been worried sick about you. You just left. I didn't even know you had a problem. I thought you might be dead. Are you caught up in some criminal activity? Were you running drugs for some cartel, and now you've been in hiding? Because that's really the only thing that can explain it..."

"That's not what this is, but seriously Hayley I need some warm clothes. I'm freezing."

She started the car and turned the AC off. "It's pretty warm out here."

"It was really cold when I got wet."

CHAPTER 29

 She drove to her house, and I went straight for the shower dropping the hundred pounds of wet woolen clothing into a sodden pile on the floor. I stood in the warm water. I shampooed. Hayley had the best-smelling, nothing but the best, products. I lathered soap all over my body.

Four months? Had I been gone four whole months? It had just been a few days, a few nights. But then I had traveled through time; how long would that take? I checked my armpits — recently shaven, barely any hair. My legs were in the same state. Three days worth of growth maybe. Not two months worth.

I felt a lot better. The pain wasn't as sharp. I toweled off. Hayley knocked and passed me a stack of clothes. A pair of soft, really soft, not scratchy sweatpants. A big oversized, also soft, rugby shirt. A pair of underwear that fit. I found some tinted cream in a drawer and patted it on the bruises on my cheek and my neck. The bruises were light, but I didn't want to have to talk about them. I wrapped my hair up in the towel and emerged in the living room. Hayley was in the kitchen. "Want a beer? Wait, can you have beer? I mean, rehab — want a soda?"

"I want a beer. Can I have an aspirin too? My whole everything hurts. Also some ice water. Yeah, ice water. You know, I'm famished. Do you have anything to eat?"

She said, "Yeah, um. . ." and opened the refrigerator to look. Then said, "Not much, let me call Michael, what do you want?"

"McDonalds."

She called. "Can you stop and bring food for Kaitlyn, from Mackydoos?. . . I know. . . Yeah." Her voice dropped to a whisper. "I know, it looks like she hasn't eaten. . . I know. . . okay see you in a few." She tossed the phone casually on the side table and dropped to the end of the couch. I placed the beer and the ice water on the coffee table, downed the aspirins, swigged water, and then sat on the couch.

But then I wobbled. "Can I lie down?" And before she could answer I had my head in her lap. "Four months?"

"Kaitlyn, you're freaking me out, girlfriend. Yes, four months." Her hand rested on my shoulder.

"What day is it?"

"Friday, January 5th."

"I missed Christmas..."

"Yeah and New Years and Halloween. Where were you?"

"Scotland, but it's a whole crazy story, and you aren't going to want to believe me, but you have to, okay?"

Her eyes drew down. "Um, okay. Sure." She got up and went to the hall closet for a blanket and spread it over me. Then she pulled my head up and sat under me depositing my head onto her lap again. I could have dozed with the blanket tucked under my chin, almost the right temperature, Hayley's hand on my shoulder, beer filling me warm and delicious. But instead I needed to talk.

"So why don't I have a house anymore?"

Hayley said, "When you disappeared like that, Zach told everyone you checked yourself into some kind of hippy-dippy spiritual away camp in Nepal or something. And that you would be back. But then six weeks passed, and no one knew what to do. Your mom and dad decided to lay off the staff and close up the house."

I rubbed my temples looking up at the ceiling. "Mom and Dad laid off the staff?"

"Yeah. So where were you? Where's Magnus? Did he do something to you?"

"No. He didn't do anything." I sat up and wrapped the blanket around my shoulders, feet tucked under me, bundled, head poking out the top.

"So you were in rehab for four months. And now you're back in some crazy get up, sopping wet, starving. What happened?"

"If I tell you something, about where I was, you're going to think it's crazy. That I'm crazy, but hear me out. Okay?"

Hayley's face was already skeptical. I was in a full panic about my house, my stuff, and Magnus might be right behind me. If he survived. If he got the extra vessel. He also might be dead, but I couldn't think about that. What if he was walking home right now and his home was gone?

Grabbing his arm before we left continued to be a monumental mistake.

"Promise you'll hear me out before you decide I'm crazy, okay? So you know how Magnus always seemed like he was from the past? He was. From the past. He's actually from the eighteenth century and—"

Hayley said, "So it's not that he's into cosplay—"

"No, he's not cosplaying."

Hayley, squinted her eyes.

"I know it sounds totally crazy, but this is the truth."

"It's impossible, Katie. You do sound crazy. Totally crazy. Time travel is a storyline in a Marvel movie. It's fiction—"

"It happened. That's all I can say. Magnus and his mother

came forward in time using a vessel — wait, it's in my purse on the bathroom floor. Can you get it?"

"Sure." She returned a second later with my bag. I sat up and pawed through the sopping wet contents. My phone was dripping wet, plus cracked from when I dropped it on the stairwell in the castle. The last fingers touching these things belonged to Lord Delapointe rifling through it three hundred years ago.

My drivers license wasn't here, great. I would have to go to the DMV.

I held up the vessel on the palm of my hand. "This is it. If I hold it and say a series of numbers, I'll travel back and forth from Scotland, 1700s to here, 2017."

"2018," corrected Hayley.

I groaned and put my head back on the couch.

Hayley took the vessel from my palm and turned it over and over investigating it. "So Magnus came here from the past..."

"And when he disappeared after our wedding, that was to go back to Scotland. Those men he was fighting in the restaurant—"

"They're also from the past."

"Exactly. And then Magnus was going to go to the past again, and I touched his arm. I was dragged there with him. And that's where I've been."

"You spent four months in the 18th century?"

"I spent three days in the 18th century, and it was plenty. Oh my god, it was..." I let my voice trail off with a shiver.

"I'm not saying I believe you, not at all, but if it's awful why does he keep going back?"

"There are more of these. In the wrong hands they're very dangerous."

"So again, not believing you, but please don't tell Michael any of this. He's six weeks into a history class and thinks he's an expert on anything that ever happened, and he'll want to go help."

My jaw dropped. "He's taking classes?"

"Yes, and any excuse to drop some fact about history or philosophy into any conversation — aargh, if I didn't love him, I'd kill him."

"Well, I'm not telling him and no one wants to go help. It sucks Hayley. It hurts so bad to travel through time. Like really. Like you die and you're yanked back to life. I don't want to go back again. You'll have to believe me. Plus, like I said, like I keep saying, I was only there for three days."

"*Really?*"

"Really, three nights in the eighteenth century. That's it. And four months are gone. I know it sounds crazy. I woke up in a marsh after time-jumping from the early eighteenth century. Look at the clothes. Look at the weird vessel I'm carrying. Think about everything you know about my husband, Magnus. I can't explain it, but it's true."

She took a deep breath.

"Zach believes me."

"He does? When did you tell him?"

"He figured it out, before I left."

"Well, he did get all the brains in the family."

"Hayley, Michael is going to college."

She waved it away with her hand. "Whatever, a couple of classes at the city college. I'm very proud, blah blah blah."

"You are too proud, I can see it in your face."

She smiled down at the blanket. "I am. It's really great."

"So, do you believe me?"

"I don't, not really. It's a harebrained story, but it's way more believable than Magnus, as hot as he is, doesn't know anything about the world. He should be a trash-talking f-boy, but he's not — clearly he's been living under a rock or traveled here from the past. So I don't believe you, but I can admit that it's probably true. I just need more proof. Can I be a cautious believer? Not sure?"

"Yeah, I mean I'm asking for a lot."

"So where is he now?"

"I went on an information gathering mission to Lady Mairead's castle. Her husband Lord Delapointe killed one of my guards and then held me captive. Magnus turned himself in and there was a big fight and I was able to escape –"

"Man, Magnus is such a bad ass."

"Are you listening? I was captive. I almost got murdered. I saw someone get murdered. I punched the guy with my keys in my fingers, like this..." I dug my keys out of my purse, brought them up, and then dropped them back. "There's still blood on them."

Hayley said, "No way." She picked up my bag to see the keys. "Crap, there's blood on the keys."

"I punched the guy and then swung something heavy, like a candlestick, against his head. While I was doing that, Magnus was fighting two guards. He yelled, 'Run!' So I ran. I ran through the castle, out to the woods, found where Magnus hid the vessel, and now I'm back here."

Hayley sighed, "Your clothes are way old."

"And remember, I'm rich because my husband has the largest collection of rare antique coins and jewels from the turn of the eighteenth century. They're in pristine condition. Like they were crafted yesterday. Also, Lady Mairead collected paintings, I haven't had them appraised yet, but they look to me like they were painted by Picasso."

"Picasso? Like *the* Picasso? He's not that old."

"I think Lady Mairead was jumping to different time periods."

She looked at me skeptically, then took a swig of beer. "You don't know if Magnus is okay?"

"Nope. He might have died. He also might have survived but doesn't have a way to get home because I took our only vessel. So many things might have happened, and I won't know anything until he comes back." I laid my head back in her lap and stretched down the couch.

"I'm sorry sweetie, that really sucks."

"I left him behind. I didn't want to, but I promised him I would do what he told me to do. Basically, I owed him to do it. I had to prove I trusted him, and he could trust me."

She scoffed, "You're the most trusting person I know."

"It's a different kind of trust. I'm loyal, but I also have a mind of my own. I don't like to follow orders. As you know."

"He's giving you orders?"

"Shit got pretty life and death. Someone needed to tell me what to do. But Magnus takes orders too. You know me Hayley; you've known me all my life. I'm not making this up. I'm not in a cult. I haven't gone and become a brainwashed bride to some lunatic abuser. I just — *Magnus*."

She frowned down at the vessel in her hand. "So where did this come from?"

"Magnus's father gave it to Lady Mairead."

"So is his dad from the future, or is he an alien?"

I looked at Hayley dumbfounded. "Um I don't really know.""

"You never asked?"

"There wasn't a lot of talking going on, like I said — murder, rape, mayhem."

"Rape?"

"Yeah. Shit got really real." I looked down at my hands. "This guy, he attacked me. He was on me and I couldn't breathe and he was ripping my—"

"Aw honey..." Hayley took my hand and squeezed it. "Are you okay? Is that the bruise on your face?"

I nodded. "But a lot happened since then. A lot. Somehow the three-hundred-years thing made it fade into memory pretty fast."

Hayley opened her purse and took out a little compact with cream foundation and began patting the makeup sponge against the bruise on my cheek. I pointed at my neck. She made a tsk noise and patted cream over that bruise too. "What did Magnus do?" Her voice was quiet, serious.

"He tried to kill him."

She returned the sponge to the compact and hugged my shoulders. "If you need to talk about it, you can, I'm listening."

"Thank you babe. I will if I need to, but right now there are bigger things to deal with. And to answer your question, I haven't asked where the tech is from. I have no idea. It must be from the future though because alien technology would be totally ridiculous."

"The boys will be here any minute now, you just, you can't tell them, sweetie. You can't tell anyone about this. You were in rehab. Your husband is working in Scotland. The world isn't ready for the story you're telling. I don't know what kind of trouble it could cause, but I imagine it would be big, big trouble. The kind that requires helicopters and hazmat suits. You saw ET, you know. And you don't think you have the plague do you?"

"The plague, god no. That's like a whole other century. You should let Michael explain it to you later tonight." I mimicked their lovemaking sounds, "Oh, oh, Michael, oh god, Michael, tell me about the plagues. Oh Hayley, the plagues were like, *centuries* ago."

"Very funny."

"Yeah, now that you're screwing a college boy your sex life will have to get more educational."

She rolled her eyes.

James and Michael walked in.

"Shit Katie, what the hell is this, jeezus I thought you were dead." James plopped the bags of food and a giant coke on the table in front of me, gestured for me to raise my feet, sat, and offered his lap for my feet to settle on. He dug in the bag and handed me food. He had ordered two Big Macs for me which seemed like it might almost be enough. As long as fries happened too.

Everyone watched me scarf down the burgers until finally I felt enough normal to be able to talk. James asked, "When did you get back, and where the hell have you been?"

I began a bullshit tirade: "I went to this spiritual retreat, in Nepal to help me, because I was living in LA you know. All the celebrities are doing it. So I went, and you're not going to believe this, I had no idea when I signed up, but it was a 'no contact with the outside world' retreat. And I already signed the paperwork."

Michael said, "Is that even legal?"

"I don't know, but the hot springs were totally worth it." I glanced at Hayley. She had her beer bottle pressed to her lips.

James said, "You've been there for four months. Why would you do anything like that for that long?"

"I was meditating, getting in touch with myself. Apparently I was very very lost."

James's eyes squinted suspiciously. "You look like hell."

"Thanks man. That means a lot. The food was vegan, so that might be part of it. And my trip back was absolute hell."

"Vegan meditation, sounds like hell on earth. We need a bacon party pronto."

"True that." I slurped a huge slurp of coke. "God that tastes good."

Michael took a big swig of a beer. "Why did Hayley find you on the side of the road?"

I rubbed my temples dramatically. "Ugh, I had to take a four-hour bus ride down a mountain that turned into a fourteen hour bus ride from hell. I missed my flight, had a layover in Dallas, barely slept in two days and then my taxi driver from the airport didn't speak any English and dropped me on the side of the road.

If Hayley hadn't come along just then I don't know what I was going to do."

Michael said, "See, James, told you there was an explanation."

"You said Katie was undead and came back as a zombie."

"Now I know the facts, Occam's Razor, the simplest explanation is usually true."

I said, "Occam's Razor?"

Hayley stifled a giggle.

"I learned about it in my philosophy class just last week."

"Hayley mentioned you're taking classes, that's awesome Michael."

"I decided to go to school. This minimum wage stuff is for the birds. Plus, if Hayley and I are going to get married—"

"What — you're getting married?" I scrambled up and jumped on Hayley throwing my arms around her neck. "When did he ask you, what did he say, oh my god."

Hayley laughed. "One night he said, 'You know we should get married someday, just not now, but someday.' And I said, 'Yeah, sounds good.' But we haven't planned anything yet. But he's enrolled at the community college now, so yeah..."

I pretended to wipe a tear. "It's the most romantic thing I've ever heard. And also, I'm so happy for you both."

James said, "So where's Magnus. He didn't come back with you?"

I shook my head slowly. "No, he still has business in Scotland. It could be awhile." I looked around the room. Hayley was looking away, awkwardly, Michael was oblivious. James's eyes squinted, as if he didn't believe me.

Michael said, "Too bad Quentin isn't here, he's been worried sick about you guys."

"Where is he?"

"Doing time for 'failure to report' for that 'discharging a gun in city limits' citation he got last summer. He has four weeks left."

"Oh no, poor Quentin. Did he have a lawyer?"

"Nah, and no job, no house. He's been drinking a lot. His parole officer was warning him. Trouble was bound to happen."

"What about Zach and Emma, and oh my god, the baby?"

Hayley looked over at Michael. "He and Emma aren't really talking to us at the moment. So we don't really know."

"Why?" I rubbed my temples, not sure I wanted to hear.

Michael said, "Because when they lost their jobs with you Zach went back to temping but Hayley couldn't find him anything permanent. He's staying on a friend's couch working as a line cook. Emma is living with her parents in Gainesville. Zach is freaking out and mad at everyone. He kept telling your dad you promised him a job and health insurance and—"

Hayley added, "Your mom said she would have the police escort them off the property."

I groaned. "Oh my god. I did, I promised them. Magnus did. Magnus is going to be so upset when he finds out Zach is out on the streets. I only —" I stopped myself before I said, 'grabbed my husband's arm', and continued, "I just wanted to go away on a spiritual retreat, and now my whole life is falling apart."

James said, "Let that be a lesson, nothing good comes of ditching your friends for months of meditation with no contact. I mean seriously, you scared us."

"I'm sorry about that. It won't happen again." I raised up and squiggled my hair into a messy bun. Hayley, without being asked, handed me a hair-band off her wrist.

"I need a piece of paper and a pen to make a list. First, I need to kick my parents' asses. Seriously, their daughter goes into rehab, and they fire all her employees?"

"You didn't leave instructions. They didn't know what to do."

"True, but still. Second, lease my house again. Third, beg

Chef Zach to come back to work. Fourth, spring Quentin from jail."

James said, "You need another beer, this is a long list."

He got up to go to the bathroom and returned a moment later. "What the hell is up with the giant brown soggy dress?"

Hayley and I looked at each other. I said, "Oh that, that was for a joke. I wanted to look just like Lady Mairead when I came back to freak you guys out, but after that trip home I lost my sense of humor."

CHAPTER 30

The next morning I woke up with a spectacular hangover. The kind that comes not so much from drinking, though there was plenty of that, but from other chemical issues — like too nervous, upset, not enough sleep, not enough nutrition, time jumping, excruciating pain, adrenaline, close to frost-bitten, nerves on edge. The hangover was going to happen, the beer simply ushered it in.

Hayley drove me to my parents's house after I called them to tell them I was coming, because I figured it would be easier than showing up and giving them a heart attack. I just played it cool on the phone, "Oh yeah, I was on a spiritual retreat, yeah sort of like rehab, but I'm back, Hayley picked me up from the airport," that kind of thing. And when I walked up to my parents's house I gave myself a big pep talk: *Play it cool, pretend like it's normal to disappear for four months. It was rehab. Talk fast and sure and play it easy.*

I walked on in. "Mom, Dad?"

Mom rushed out with her hands on her hips. "Rehab? Seriously? Do you know what people are whispering about you? That you've had a breakdown. That you're locked up under surveillance, twenty-four-hour." I dropped down into one of the chairs at the kitchen table.

"Well I wasn't. It was actually more like a spiritual retreat. I got in touch with my Ching and my Yangalang. It's all the rage in Los Angeles."

Dad humphed and returned to his activity, stuffing veggies into a blender.

Mom said, "Well, we were worried sick. I didn't know what to tell everyone. Why would you go to one of those places? You don't have any problems."

I rolled my eyes, feeling fifteen again, lying to mom. "If you remember, mom, I seem to have anger issues. It's one of the reasons my whole life fell apart last summer. So I went to handle it, get my Shabbylinguoi in order. You know, with meditation and chanting."

Mom looked like she thought I was crazy. "I haven't heard of any of that."

"It's very hip, very right now, very oh look, the actress who may or may not play on Iron Man may have been there."

Mom said, "Really? Did you meet her?"

"I can't say, but I met some royalty, that was interesting."

"So it wasn't one of those twelve-step programs, right? You won't have to go to meetings?"

"Nope, they say I'm clean, pure, and my Sim-gushers are in order again. So besides a weekly massage, there's not much I need to do."

Mom shook her head, "Well, you are lucky, my friend Camilla is an alky, and she says she still battles with it." Mom did air quotes with her fingers around 'alky' and 'still battles.'

I joked, "Well, that's alcohol. My problem was imbalances in my Superstruction, so there's a difference."

"Ah, probably. That does sound good. It was like a spa?"

I nodded. "Just like a spa. Exactly like one." Dad pushed the grind button on the juicer for a moment, and we quieted because it was so very loud. When he finished, he dipped a finger in and declared it delicious.

"So where's Magnus?"

"He's still on the spiritual retreat. He doesn't have anger issues but wanted to complete his Fingway training."

She waved her hand dismissing my comment. "It was just a marriage of convenience anyway. I suppose you'll have to get used to living apart a great deal of time. We haven't spent any time with him since the wedding. It would be nice to see him again. You know, he reminds me of that Outlander guy, what's his name...?"

"You know, he gets that all the time. So, speaking of my anger issues, why did you close down my house and fire my staff while I was away?"

"Well, it was just wasting money. There was no need for it, right dear?" She looked toward my dad who was pouring two glasses of vegetable juice. He placed them in front of me and mom. It looked disgusting, like I might barf. Mom drank hers down.

Dad poured a third into a mug for himself. "Just pouring money down the drain. We had to strengthen your portfolio for long term growth. He licked the big wooden spoon he was using.

Mom added, "And frankly, that Zach person was not a good employee. I think you'll do good to start over—"

"Chef Zach was an excellent employee. I'm not starting over, you had no right to—"

"Well dear, you didn't leave us instructions, or even tell us where you were going. We just assumed—"

"Here's the thing, I did leave word where I had gone and what the instructions were. I told Zach I was going on a spiritual retreat and that he would continue to be employed while I was gone. Did he tell you that?"

Mom opened and closed her mouth twice. Dad said, "He did, but we didn't know he was speaking with authority."

"Well he was. He was hired by Magnus. I will need to hire him again because Magnus will be furious he's gone."

"He was insolent to me and your father."

"What did he say?"

"That he wouldn't leave. We'd have to force him out."

"Well, he was doing what I told him to do. Not very insolent, it's just you disagreed."

"What were we to do, keep them employed even though you weren't there?"

"Don't I have the money for it?"

Dad said, "You do for now, but not if you pay people to sit around. You need to toughen up."

I sighed. "That may be true, but also, Zach is a special case. He and Emma have a value that Magnus is willing to pay for even if he's not there. So yeah, I just wanted to let you know that I'm back, and I'll be taking over the reigns of the household again. Thank you for your work on my behalf."

Mom said, "That's fine dear. You'll see that we paid ourselves a salary for management in your absence."

I bit my lips, close to raging, but deciding that might blow my whole story. Instead I nodded with my lips between my teeth looking like a psychopath. "Yeah, of course you did. You paid yourself a salary. I'm super happy about that. Chef Zach is living on a couch and you and Dad got an extra paycheck. That's awesome Mom. Okay." I stood up. "Is there anything I need to sign to get my house back?"

Mom jumped up to gather paperwork. Dad looked indifferent. He began to wash cups, leaving mine, untouched, in front of me. Mom hustled back in, "I'm glad you came back when you did. I was beginning to wonder what to do if your lease came up in a couple of months." She put the lease in front of me, the house keys, and then an extra keyring.

"What's this?"

"Your stuff has been moved into storage. There's the paperwork."

"Awesome Mom, perfect."

I stood to go. "Dad, how's Grandma?"

He turned. "Oh that's right, you almost missed the move. We decided she couldn't live on her own anymore, so we've applied to move her to an assisted-living place."

"What? Where?"

Mom said, "In Maine, near where she lives now, so she has plenty of friends around."

"When?"

"Next month."

"I want to go when you move her."

I slid all the keys and paperwork up and made to leave. "If, in the future, I go away for any length of time, I would like to have a manager set up. Someone to run my household and finances in my absence. What kind of paperwork would I need to fill out?"

Dad said, "That would be an administrator. Your mother and I would be happy to—"

"Yeah, I'll get a lawyer. Really great seeing you guys again."

"Hope you can come to dinner sometime next weekend. We're booked until then."

I found myself bustling out the door and then returning a second later. "Um, where's my car?"

"Magnus's mustang? Oh it's in the garage."

~

I took deep breaths sitting in the driver's seat of the Mustang. I only had to do a million things to put my household back together. Then I had to wait for Magnus.

I had been gone for like three days, and it almost equaled four months. Once I opened my house again, I would need to do the math. Then I would need to guess how long it would take Magnus to get a vessel and follow me. My bag was dried stiff from the soaking yesterday. My keys still had a bloodstain on them. Gross.

I wiped it on the leg of the sweatpants and started the car.

CHAPTER 31

$\mathcal{I}$ still didn't have a phone because so far I had done all of this just to get in the front door of my house.

Next, I needed to get my stuff or at least my clothes from storage. Then I needed to talk to Zach. I opened the front door of my house.

It contained the furniture it came with. Empty, dark, too cold, lifeless, and spooky. I walked around. The dressers were all empty. Everything looked realtor-staged, and frankly I did not like being here by myself.

Okay, first I needed to talk to Zach.

～

I showed up at the place he was living unannounced. The curtain slid away from the window when I knocked, and then Zach opened the door and gruffly said, "Come in." He dropped to the couch and put on his shoes.

I stood in the middle of the room. It was dark. The television flickered. Beer cans were crumpled on the floor. A bong stood on the side table. The curtains were closed. Sheets and a pillow were rumpled on the couch.

"Where's Emma?"

He continued tying his shoes without looking up. "At her parents' house, in Gainesville. You know — this isn't really the kind of place for a pregnant girl, so yeah, I'm trying to make some money so we can get our own place."

He stood and grabbed his keys, "I need to head into work soon though, so—"

"Zach, I am so sorry. I am — I don't know how to express to you, the amount of sorry."

"Hey, that's cool. It was just a job right?"

"No, it wasn't just a job. Magnus thinks of you like family and—"

Zach jiggled the keys and looked down at me. "Yeah, well, family lets us down a lot. I'm used to taking care of my own shit. Did you need something? Is that why you came by?"

"Zach, please, sit down so we can talk, please."

He sank onto the couch without a word. I perched on the edge of the recliner beside it. Now that I had his ear for a moment I didn't know where to begin. I kind of hoped he would've been so excited to see me that he just hugged me hello and came back to work. It didn't seem like it was going that way.

He started with. "When did you get back?"

"Last night. I — I was gone for like — three days."

He looked at me with his face screwed up incredulously. "What are you talking about?"

"I went back in time to sometime in the early seventeen hundreds, and I was there for four days. I just barely escaped back here and landed in the marsh I might add — that was wet, totally sucked. And guess what? My house was all closed up. You had been laid off, and I'm really sorry."

"You feel like you were only gone for three days?"

"Yeah, that's it. I had no idea so much time was passing. And — in hindsight, I should have paperwork lawyered-up that makes sure you have a job in my absence. But the truth is there won't be another time because that? It sucked, hard, awful, death-defying."

"Where's Magnus?"

"He didn't make it out. I don't know. Last I saw of him he was fighting two men, and I don't know if he survived it. Plus, I took the only time-traveling thingamajig, so he doesn't have a way to get here — I don't mean to talk just about what I went through though — how's Emma, how's the baby?"

"They're fine, the pregnancy is going okay, but Emma's pretty stressed out. Her parents have never really liked me, so my jobless ass has been proving them right."

"You have a job. You're the private chef to Magnus Campbell and his wife, Kaitlyn. And I'll get you health insurance. I know I said I would, but I mean it. I'm going to be better at this. I'll run the place like it matters."

"It was pretty tough there. Your mom is kind of a bitch. I kept telling her you wanted me to stay on. That you wanted me and Emma to take care of the place, but she threatened to call the cops and—"

"Yeah, I know, it must have super-sucked. Do you need like extra combat pay or something? What can I do? Magnus thinks the world of you, really. I mean, I think he likes me okay, but when he's in Scotland all he talks about is your cooking and how much he misses it. And what I'm figuring out is that he hasn't really had a home, or a family. I met his stepfather, it was not good. You and I are it. Quentin. Emma. The baby — when you guys become parents. I hope he comes home, and I need you to be there when he does, because he would be really sad without you."

Zach chuckled. "He really loves my cooking, huh?"

"You know he does. This is not new information. You were right. My mom was wrong. I wish I had a crystal ball to see in the future, that I needed a contract for 'in case I disappeared for four months,' but I didn't, because crystal balls like time machines aren't based in reality. So there's this: I screwed up, and it sucked. Please come work for us again. I'll write up contracts. I'm going to behave more like a grown up, the matriarch of our family. And you can have combat pay."

"I get paid enough — it's just the job, the health insurance, some stability, a place." He looked around at the trashed apartment.

"It's yours. Just please come home. Right now. Because I'm hungry." I laughed. And Zach laughed. He checked his cell phone. I have to work. I'm a line cook. I barely make enough to pay my cell phone bill."

"Can you quit, now?"

"I should probably be a grown up and quit after my shift."

"We should probably both be grown ups, huh? Do you want me to go rescue Emma?"

"No, I'll drive down tomorrow morning. I'll go to church with her parents. It's a small thing that I've been slack about doing. Then I'll rescue her." He grinned.

"So you're saying I'm on my own tonight?"

He nodded.

"Fine," I joked. "I can make my own ice cream." I walked to the door. "Thank you for telling my folks it was rehab, that was perfect. And I really will make this up to you, I promise."

I got into my car and looked down at my list. I would need to talk to Quentin, possibly through a lawyer, and even with the best of intentions he might be stuck in jail. That would have to wait for the work week, probably.

Everyone would help me move my stuff back tomorrow. They were all busy tonight.

Hayley said I was invited if I wanted to come. I would spend a few hours in my empty house and decide how I felt about that.

CHAPTER 32

When I shoved up the door of the storage unit, I wanted to kill my mom for the tenth time since I got back. The unit was big, my stuff was piled in the middle with ample room left over. She was wasting money on this. Wasting it. My stuff could have been in my house. Guarded over by my guard. Watched over by my housemates, Zach and Emma.

The boxes were unlabeled. I pulled one toward me and looked inside. A spatula, a pile of silverware, a bowl with potpourri, plus a few items from my dresser, plus a pair of shoes and a bottle of shampoo.

I clenched my fists and screamed at the ceiling. Then I let forth a barrage of profanity, that went from simple to completely off the rails, "Fucking waste of money, stupidest thing I ever saw. Who the hell did she hire to pack my shit, has that person never seen a freaking sharpie pen? Ever? How hard is it to write a label on the outside of the box? It's like the one rule of boxing stuff. Look at this freaking box — it has a spot for writing the contents. It says 'contents.' There's no way to ignore its intent, it's a mother-fucking rule."

I shoved that box closed and ripped open another one. "Jesus Christ, it's a goddam travesty. I'm off fighting an evil overlord in the 18th century and my spices are thrown in with my hand towels. Not kitchen towels, freaking hand towels. Oh wait, what the hell is this?" I pulled up a candle stick. "Oh my god. A candlestick. With spices and hand towels. What the fuck were the packers doing, grabbing one thing from each room?"

And then I yelled again, "Arrrrghhhh!" as loud as I could. "It was my house. My stuff. My family. My husband—" and then I sat in the middle of a storage unit in Florida and cried. My tears surpassed the travesty of poorly packed boxes and grief about my poorly planned life — where was Magnus? Was he alive?

I hadn't allowed myself to really think yet. I had been trying to piece together my life, I hadn't faced the reality — my husband might not have made it.

He might have thrown his life away to save mine.

I had watched a lot of movies in my day and the guy that stays behind so the others can flee? He was sacrificing himself.

And how was I to deal with that without knowing? Just waiting? Would it be easier to tell myself he was gone forever? Would anything ever be easy again?

No, never.

Because I was a widow. By marrying someone from another century I had become a widow as soon as I spoke the vows. It was clear. Every moment with him was borrowed time, he was right about that. Had been right about that.

Whenever I closed my eyes I saw him fighting, bellowing, roaring in rage trying to kill his captors — he couldn't live through that.

And I couldn't live with the memory.

I needed to change it, to try to replace it with a better one.

His lips on my shoulder. "You are a surprise Madame Campbell."

Or his wrist tied to mine, his hands shaking, his voice rumbling above my bowed head, "I take thee Kaitlyn Sheffield. . ."

Or his chest, the feel of it under my palms telling me that his feelings for me — that I was a brutal love.

He had loved me so much and he had shown me. I might have been the luckiest person in the world for that. In all of time.

I wiped the tears from my eyes. Becoming a widow without knowing what became of your husband would be desperately hard.

It would require a list. I dug through my bag for a pen and wrote on the closest box:

One, accept the truth.

Two, pull on your big girl panties.

Three, act like a grown up.

Four, take care of the people around you.

Five, always check the sky.

I looked at the list for a few moments and then wrote:

Six, if you're checking the sky, go back through the list again.

I spent the next hour digging through the pile attempting to find enough of my things to be comfortable tonight alone in my house. I narrowed it down to three of the top boxes and stuffed them in the trunk of my Mustang. At the grocery store I bought three tubs of ice cream, two of my favorite flavors, plus a vanilla just to have, like a memorial ice cream.

I cried a bit in the freezer section of the grocery store.

Then, because I didn't have the right kitchen stuff, I went through the McDonald's drive-thru for dinner.

CHAPTER 33

My house, even with my paltry three boxes of stuff was cold and dark and empty. I put a box down in the living room and went down for another and then another. Then, last, the groceries. I placed the ice cream on a barren shelf in the freezer and then sat at the counter island in front of my bags of dinner. I unwrapped a burger and took a big bite, chewed it, and then another. The paper wrapping echoed. My chewing filled my head. My thoughts raced around and around in circles, keeping all else away. Like an echo. It reminded me of being back in time when my body echoed inside myself.

For some reason I couldn't stop thinking about Ewan's arm across my throat as I struggled to breathe, and then his throat, cut, his body slumped to the ground. His face beaten by my husband and — I dropped my head to the cold marble counter of the kitchen island, pressed, my eyes clamped, close to hyperventilating, icy cold fear crawling up my spine — I heard a noise.

The house was lit up brightly. I couldn't see outside at all. I slunk to the light switch and dimmed the interior so I could see the empty deck. Nothing.

Then I heard another noise, this one from inside the house. Someone was upstairs.

My heart raced. I crept along the wall to the kitchen drawer that used to have knives and pulled it open. Empty.

I backed up into the short hall to the laundry room. *I might find something to use as a weapon, a can of something, or* — on the counter was a heavy glass dish full of potpourri, a common scent, dubbed 'the beach'. It didn't smell like a beach at all, but I thought it was awesome.

I dumped the potpourri on the floor and held the bowl back ready to swing. I watched the stairs for whoever was coming down.

I stayed like that quietly waiting, terrified, for what seemed like hours. The noise happened again, it sounded like footsteps.

And then without a doubt, a door opening.

I had no phone. If I ran, I could get to the door and make a break for it. I walked stealthily, around the edge of the kitchen toward the front door, still holding the glass dish like a weapon. Feet descended the steps — "Who is it, who's there?" — woolen skirts — I was staring dumbfounded at my mother-in-law, her cold icy gaze glaring at me from the stairs.

"Kaitlyn Campbell, I would like a word."

"Jesus, Lady Mairead, how did you—? Where did you—?"

"I have a key. Tis my fortune that has paid for this..." She looked around distastefully. "I arrived earlier today. I am still in agony, though doing better, thank ye."

"Oh." I said dumbly. And put the glass dish back on the counter. My footsteps crunched across the kitchen floor through the spilled potpourri. "Um, why are you—where is Magnus, is he okay?"

She dismissed my question with a wave of her hand. "I have come tae have a word with ye, daughter." Her words were like ice and frankly kind of scary.

My heart was still beating in my ears.

"Magnus is gone, you will nae see him again." She ran a hand down the front of her bodice and skirt as if brushing off the bad news.

"Oh my god, is he — oh my god — I don't—" I grabbed hold of the counter to steady myself.

She walked down the steps to me. "You have done your work most effectively. Taking my fortune, ridding yourself of Magnus, stealing my vessel. A most effective theft, I am impressed at your brazenness."

"That's not — I love Magnus." I put my hand over my mouth. My limbs were shaking.

"Och, aye, love. Interesting concept, but ye, my dear — Signed. A. Contract." She slammed the handwritten contract I signed last summer down on the counter, right between my half-eaten Big Mac and a cardboard container with all my fries, now cold. My wedding contract.

"I will remind ye that the contract was with me and when you signed it I made myself clear. You would. Keep. Magnus. Here."

I chewed my lip.

"Was that nae my intent? When I told ye tae marry Magnus, was that nae what I said — for ye tae keep him here?" Her voice was loud and dangerous sounding.

I nodded.

"Answer me!"

"Yes."

She set her jaw. "Explain tae me what my intent was." She eyed me, her brow furrowed, her glare intense.

I looked away. "For me to keep Magnus here, to give him a reason to stay, to protect him."

"Tae protect him." Her eyes were so hard and cruel that I couldn't raise mine to meet them.

"I have been in hiding, and during that time I have found that my son has returned tae Scotland twice. Twice! My husband beat him. Has imprisoned him."

"I'm sorry. I tried to keep him here, but he had reasons—"

She scoffed, malevolently. "Reasons. And now ye speak tae me of love. You came tae my time and now my nephew Ewan is dead. My son Sean is imprisoned. My brother is raising an army against my husband. There will be a war." She banged a hand down on the wedding contract. "Explain how your marriage tae my son turned out so terribly for me?"

"I don't know."

"Och, aye, you don't know." She leveled her gaze.

"Is Magnus dead?"

"It dinna matter tae ye. Get used tae the fact that ye and Magnus arna tae be together anymore."

"We're married, in church. You can't decide that we can't be together —" I hated the sound of my voice. I sounded like a petulant child against a pissed off parent and while true, the stakes were so much higher.

"Magnus Campbell is dead tae ye. He has been dead now for three hundred years. You have married a ghost, and if ye wants tae continue on pretending tae be married tae a ghost then tis nae matter tae me. You shall do as ye wish. But know this, Kaitlyn Campbell, ye winna see him again."

"I — I don't... please, this is... is he alive in the 18th century? If I could just see him, I could make this better. I'll be better at it."

"Give me the vessel ye stole from Magnus." She held out her palm.

I shook my head. "No, you can't have it. He gave it to me, and I might—"

"You have one option that ye live through. And that is tae give me the vessel. I have three weapons on my person as we speak, and I am capable of using all of them. I assume ye are unarmed, else ye winna have been yielding a fancy glass bowl earlier."

My eyes flitted to the door and in one move she had my arm yanked behind my back and the sharp point of a knife at my throat. I tried to draw away, but she held me firm. "I want the vessel. Now." Her breath was hot and smelly, putrid, like death, on my cheek. Tears rolled down my face. "Please don't take it, it's the only way I can get to him if I need to."

"Exactly." Her knife pressed at my pulse on my neck.

"It's in my bag."

She released me, shoving me against a barstool.

I dug through my purse for the vessel and placed it in her palm. "Magnus gave it to me. He made me take it. He saved my life."

"Yes, a word of advice, cherish that memory. I have many memories of lost loves performing acts of chivalry for me. You will need something tae keep ye company as ye suffer long nights of widowhood. Or perhaps ye will get lucky and have a second marriage or a third. They are often far more complicated, but have their own merits. Mine have been verra useful tae me through the years. Now nae so much. But tis the penalty of being a woman, ye must handle the men of your life."

"You haven't told me if he's alive. I need to know — I..."

She dropped the vessel into the sporran-like bag she wore at her waist. "You daena need tae know anything about him. You have forfeited your claim."

"If he is alive he's going to come for me. You won't be able to stop him."

She crossed to the sliding doors and opened them. "He has no way to get to you, and you have no way to get to him." She stately walked across the deck and down the boardwalk.

"Stop, please!"

I would never ever see him. I would never know. I would never find out.

I ran after her, through the open sliding door, across the deck, and down the boardwalk. "Lady Mairead, please tell me what happened to Magnus. I don't understand. I know you're upset, but I love him. I want to protect him. If he's alive, please let me see him."

She stopped mid walk and stood for a half moment, then she turned fast and charged me with a knife. It was raised and aimed for my heart.

When I cowered she bore over me with her teeth bared. "You had a job, and ye dinna perform your duties."

She stepped forward, within striking distance, forcing me to step back, concentrating my gaze on the raised knife point.

"But because I am kind, I will spare your life. Tis as my late son, Magnus, would have wished, and it does me nae harm tae allow ye tae live in this future." She lowered the knife. "Tis easy tae allow ye tae live, because ye mean nothing."

She turned and walked down the boardwalk to the beach, her feet echoing, thud, thud, thud. It was about seven pm; the sky had gone dark already. The January winds whipped the sea grass, my hair, Lady Mairead's skirts.

I crumpled on the handrail. "Please!" But my words were whisked away behind me

As soon as Lady Mairead's feet hit the sand, she began reciting numbers. Clouds rose to the heavens, coming from the north. A wind roared like a locomotive and lightning arced from the front edge. Lady Mairead faced the storm and with a boom and a flash of light she was gone.

I collapsed to the boardwalk and sobbed.

CHAPTER 34

I called Hayley, clammy, dizzy, and about to totally freak out.

"Hey babe how you—"

"Hayley, I'm freaking out, oh my god—" I burst into tears.

"Oh sweetie, I'm so sorry. I'm so sorry this is happening."

"Lady Mairead just came. She took the vessel thingy, and I'm a widow. Magnus is gone and I don't know what to do with it..."

"Oh Katie, I'm — look, I'm at this thing. I'm at dinner with Michael's parents, but I'll come as soon as it's over. I'll stay the night. Can you hold on that long?"

I nodded, tears streaming down my face.

"Can you?"

"I don't know..."

"Okay, good enough. I'm on my way."

She hung up and it was darkness and sadness but at least I knew someone was coming.

CHAPTER 35

*H*ayley bustled in and took over the mood. She opened a twelve pack on the counter and shoved beers into the fridge. "What did Lady Mairead do?"

"She was here, in the house. She threatened me. She took the vessel. She told me Magnus was dead, and I would never see him again."

She raised up and looked at me. "Did she say he was dead, or that you'd never see him again. Those are two totally different things."

"I don't know, it was all so confusing, and there was a knife at my throat and—"

"She held a knife at your throat? What the hell..." She brought two beers to the couch and opened one for me and one for her. She sat quietly for a long moment. "Was she angry or sad?"

"Angry."

"Hmmmmmmm." She pushed her feet under one end of the blanket, her legs wrapped around mine. "So what do you think she was doing here?"

I looked at her quizzically. Much like Magnus looked when he was confused by me.

"I mean, why would she come? *You* didn't kill Magnus, her husband did."

"She blames me for bringing him there."

"He's a grown ass man, his magical vessel. I blame *him* for bringing *you* there. Do you want ice cream? I saw that was the only thing in your freezer."

I nodded and she went to the kitchen and asked, "What have you eaten tonight?" She eyed the McDonald's bags suspiciously.

"That."

"Katie, this is not real food. You lived in Los Angeles, right? Can't you do better? If you're depressed and going through time-jumping, I think you're supposed to watch your nutrition, get lots of vitamins. You could get the freaking plague."

"I think salads make me depressed."

She looked at me with her hands on her hips. "Are you still wearing the clothes I loaned you last night?"

I nodded.

"Okay, so first you'll take a shower. Because last night's was just the first shower of many that you need to get the fifth century off you."

"Eighteenth century."

"It's literally the same thing, and you know it. It's not here, is what I'm saying, so you need to get here. That's what I mean."

I said, "Maybe I don't want to take a shower. Maybe if I take a shower, I'm saying good bye to everything forever. Maybe there's still some Magnus dust on me and that's all I have left."

Her face grew stern.

I added, "Maybe, you don't know."

She looked deflated. "I don't, that's true — look, are you comfortable? Maybe that's all you need to do right now; what do I know?"

She twisted the tops off two more beers, dove into the freezer and pulled out the gallons of chocolate chunk chocolate surprise ice cream. And lifted their lids. She pulled open a drawer. "Where are your utensils?"

"Everything is in storage."

She groaned, pulled open every drawer until she found a lone spoon and fork. She stuck them both into the top of the ice cream. Then she hooked the beers under her arm and balanced the lot of full cartons and bottles to me on the couch.

"I just don't get why she would threaten you if he's dead. When she was talking, was she talking about her son like he was dead, or was she trying to scare you?"

"I think she was trying to scare me."

"Why would she do that if Magnus is dead? She could have just told you that Magnus was dead and told you to give her back the box. But she didn't, she scared you. Why?"

"Because she said I would never get to see him again."

"See?"

"You think he's alive?"

"I think he's alive or the conversation with your mother-in-law would have been totally different."

"Magnus is alive..."

"Yep."

"But my mother-in-law said I'll never get to see him again."

"Well, Magnus doesn't seem like the kind of guy who will let a bitch like Lady Mairead stand between him and your sexy ass."

I smiled sadly. "He does love me."

"Exactly, does, not did, *does*. He's alive, girlfriend, this is good news."

I ate a big bite of chocolate chunky ice cream with a vein of caramel running through it and let it cool down my insides.

"God, she is a scary bitch."

"You aren't the first person in the history of time with a scary bitch mother-in-law, but it might be a first to have one that is three hundred years old and can still hold a knife to your throat."

"She stole the vessel. I should have fought her."

"What were you going to do with it? You weren't actually going to go back in time and look for him?"

"I don't know, I might have, if he didn't come soon..."

"How would that even work? I mean, it's like horses, right? Barbarians, no phones? What would be your plan?"

"I don't know, it was just nice to have the option."

"Remember when you were a kid at Disney World and your mom would tell you, 'If you get lost...'" She rolled her hand asking me to continue.

"Stay where you are."

"Exactly—"

"But am I the one that's lost?"

"You are. Because of the barbarians and the lack of phones. Let him find you. He knows where you live. Stay put."

"I guess you're right."

"I am, I'm always right."

I laughed, feeling much, much better than an hour ago. "And he always calls me mo reul-iuil. It means my North Star."

She grinned widely, wickedly. "Your vajayjay will guide him."

"You are a piece of work."

She took a bite of ice cream and said with her mouth full, "I've seen how he looks at you. When you're in the room, he doesn't see anyone else. His eyes follow you. He loves you so much. He'll come to you I know it."

"I'll just wait and eat ice cream and cry in these old sweatpants until he comes."

She shook her head. "You are a sad case."

"I feel so much better. Thank you for coming. What did I make you miss?"

"The tenth of like a million discussions about what our wedding will be like. Michael's mom is a nut job. She has always believed Michael can do no wrong. It's like she's given up on Zachary. She won't even talk about how he's about to have a baby. It's out of wedlock so I guess she thinks it doesn't count."

"Zach is picking up Emma tomorrow morning. He's bringing her here. He'll be working for me again."

"That's good. I'm glad you'll have someone here." Our legs were crossed in the middle of the couch, a blanket across us both, our bowls tucked on our tummies. The only difference between us was that I looked like hell and she was all done up, her hair and makeup to perfection.

"I'm glad you and Michael are getting married, can I be your maid of honor?"

"That goes without saying. Your main job will be to keep my mother-in-law out of my hair."

We both chuckled. It was funny that her mother-in-law problems were small scale compared to mine. "She should be nice to you. You're the best thing that ever happened to him."

"True that. I think he might be a school teacher now, instead of a busboy. Like a real life grown-up school teacher."

I smiled but then my face, like my insides, fell. A tear rolled down my face. "She said I would never see him again. What if she's right?"

Hayley swigged some beer. "I don't know sweetie. You'll just have to have faith. It's not going to be easy."

"Yeah... speaking of hard. I forgot a toothbrush, plus I'm super sleepy—" I yawned. "Are you leaving?"

"Nope, I'm staying the night. A good old fashioned sleepover. So if you fall asleep first... watch out."

I curled up. "Goodnight."

"Goodnight, Kaitlyn. It's going to be okay. He's alive, I just know it."

CHAPTER 36

I woke up at about 2:00 am in a cold sweat. I had been having a dream — I thought back through it: darkness, Magnus with blood running down his face, pressure on my neck, screams filling my ears, Lady Mairead's bared teeth in a grin. These would not be easy images to get past.

Hayley was sleeping, mouth open at the other end of the couch, arm dangling off the side, slightly snoring. I pushed the heavy comforter down and crept quietly to my master bathroom. I peed, thinking about the chamber pot and Magnus joking about our frosted glass door. I had been so furious with Magnus at the castle, absolutely pissed, but his care and attention lacing my dress, his forehead pressed to mine, his oath to follow me into the woods and live in a tent outside my cottage... I had forgiven him. It was the everyday gestures that convinced me to. The simple conversation. And the truth — he was always and forever and would be — *ever*.

I groaned when I realized that there wasn't any toilet paper. Whose job was it to do the restocking? Not mine. I was going to kill my mom.

I tiptoed through the dark house to the kitchen and ran my fingertips down the marble counter. It felt like it had only been a few days since my ass had been here, my legs spread before my husband. Just six days ago or something like that. Yet so much time, space, air, had passed through the house since then; the counter had long forgotten.

Just me. I remembered.

I poured a big glass of water, no ice because the dispenser would wake up Hayley, and leaned on the counter. I stared out across the dark room and a memory slammed into me.

It hit me hard like a punch to the gut.

The kind that knocks out your air with a gust. So forcefully that hyperventilation was soon to follow.

A memory that was clean and sure and unmistakable — and felt so terribly, unbelievably true.

I was living in Los Angeles, about two years ago. Braden and I were celebrating a big milestone — was it a hundred thousand followers, two hundred, or the half million mark? At the time it seemed important.

The show that day had been big. I had thrown my heart into it, a v-log about throwing an Oscars-watching party. I basically planned a party, orchestrated it, and scripted an episode interesting enough for people to want to tune in.

I gave Braden a list of things to buy, hoping to involve him in the plans, but he couldn't find a few of the things, important things, and returned home without them. He said, "I figured you'd be able to work around it."

And I took that as a compliment and did find a way, but really, by the time we uploaded the video, I was exhausted. Our witty repertoire during the video was mostly him being charming and funny, and me being harried and one step away from freaking out.

But after the upload of that video we were celebrating. The viewers thought we were delightful and everything else fell away. I forgave Braden because that was 'the way he was,' not interested in the details. He brought the fun to the team.

But what I really wanted to do was go to bed.

He wanted to go out and celebrate more.

He tweeted that he was going to take me to a fancy club in West Hollywood that night. Our fans thought that was so romantic.

So a bit later, after I rubbed some lip color on, glammed my eyes with a smoky look to mask my exhaustion, and slipped into a tiny black dress with glamorous sparkly high heels, I found myself sitting across from Braden in a very hip, three-thousand-dollar-a-table nightclub. There were about twelve other people with us, barely acquaintances, most of them beautiful models and gorgeous men I should have flirted with.

But I was really, really into Braden those days.

I made up for my exhaustion by drinking too much and eating my way through a lot of appetizers. At one point the models asked us to dance, and Braden practically dragged me to the dance floor. We danced in a big group, girls, beautiful girls gyrating all around us. It was awesome, sexy, and completely jealous-making and infuriating — such was a night out celebrating in Los Angeles. The cool thing was, we were making it. Braden and I were becoming the kind of people who were followed, who commanded expensive tables, who gyrated amongst beautiful women on dance floors. Who went out because their twitter followers might want to see them.

This was all good news—

We returned to our table. I was leaned to my left speaking to one of the very handsome men. His name was like Lucious or something which was exactly right. He had an Italian accent and kissable jawline. I laughed a sparkling laugh at something inane he said—

There was a small tap on my shoulder. "Pardon me, Madame?" The voice was low, rumbling, a bass that vibrated my insides.

I turned, looked up, and there was a man — his hair was light, though he could only be described as dark. He was handsome, actually very hot. In a way that made him seem commanding. All the other men at the table suddenly looked like too-young 'pretty boys'. He seemed settled, intent, serious, and important.

I shifted to straighten my back. "Yes?"

"Madame, my name is Magnus Campbell. Would it be possible tae have a private word with ye?" He was wearing a dark linen shirt stretched across his broad shoulders with dark pants, adding to his overall darkness. He was definitely too mysterious to follow into an alley. I glanced across the table at Braden, sitting between two beautiful models, eyeing the stranger jealously.

"Um, no, I mean, why?"

He looked at me for a moment. His eyes intense — it was as if he was looking into me, talking to me, telling me something, like he knew me, down deep.

"Um... do we know each other?" I wasn't sure what else to say.

He shook his head slowly. "Nae, of course..." He continued to look at me.

I glanced over at Braden who was beginning to glare.

The stranger said, "I have found ye on the computer." He ran his hand through his hair, seeming nervous.

I decided to help. "Are you a fan of my videos?"

"Aye, I am a fan of ye." He removed an envelope from his pocket, red, square, thick, sealed. "I have heard ye are from Amelia Island?"

"I am. Are you from there?" I wanted to kick myself. Clearly he wasn't from Amelia Island; he was from Scotland or something. But his whole intense *thing* made the music, the crowds, my logic fall away.

One of the models to my far right leaned forward and giggled. "Is he a stalker? Are you being stalker-ed?" She giggled and immediately stopped caring, returning to the conversation at the other end of the table.

The stranger looked uncomfortable. He shifted his gaze down to the envelope and then back to me. "I have a message for a woman who lives on Amelia Island. I was wondering if ye would deliver it for me?"

Braden leaned across the table. "A message — why don't you just mail it?" He asked me, "Is this guy bothering you?"

I said, "Come on, Braden, he's not bothering me, he just—" I asked the stranger, "Why don't you just mail it?"

"I daena have a way tae send it tae her. Tis verra important. I have lost her."

The model from my right returned to our conversation again. "Is this like those mixed connections things?"

Another model clapped her hands. "Oh my god, I love those! Are you in love with someone, and you don't know how to find her? This is so awesome!"

By this time the whole table gave the stranger their full attention.

"Tis much like that."

I said, "But I'm not going back to Amelia Island any time soon. Are you expecting me to search for her for you? I'm not sure I—"

"Nae, I will keep searching. I was thinking ye could keep this letter, and when ye go back tae Amelia island, if ye met her..."

"It might be at least a year before I go back. I really think the internet will be faster."

He shook his head slowly. "I am nae looking for faster. I would like ye tae keep this letter inside your undergarment drawer, just in case ye meet her. Then please give it tae her."

The model to my right giggled. "Your undergarment drawer!"

I looked around the table, then back at the stranger. "Well, this is definitely mysterious. Okay, I'll hold on to the letter for you until I return to Amelia Island. Hopefully I'll meet her for you, but also it won't matter because you'll have already found her, right?"

"Aye. I am trying verra hard tae get tae her." He stood still, not moving, looking down at the envelope in his hands.

"What's her name?"

He handed me the envelope. In an old fashioned cursive with fanciful curves and lines, it read, *Mrs. Magnus Campbell.*

I laughed. "She's your wife, or your mother?"

"My wife."

"Now hold on a moment, am I getting in the middle of something? Does she not want to be found?"

"She loves me verra much and wants me tae find her."

The model to my right giggled and said, "It's so romantic! So like a year from now his wife has a stranger come up to her with a love letter from her husband — it's like a time machine, a message from the past—"

"Oh my god, Magnus is looking for me. Hayley! Wake up Hayley!" I rushed to the couch tripping over my shoes and dropped to my knees beside Hayley's face. "Wake up."

"Wha—huh? What time is it?"

"Two-twenty in the morning. Hayley, I have a new memory. It's the weirdest feeling in the world, like brain damage just occurred and something that never happened to me just appeared in my brain. It happened to me, now — oh my god, it's so weird."

"First, slow down, let me wrap my brain around how early it is." Hayley smacked her lips together and yawned. Then she pulled herself to a sitting position, yawned again, nabbed her old beer on the coffee table and took a swig. Then grimaced. "That tastes terrible, be a sweetie and get me a new one."

I jumped up, rushed to the refrigerator, grabbed a beer, unscrewed the top, and brought it to her. "Like two years ago or something I went out to dinner with Braden, we were celebrating something, and this all one hundred percent happened, all of it. But just now I was thinking about that day, I don't know why, I mean I haven't thought about that day in forever because it was so lame and uneventful—"

Hayley said, "Girlfriend you are manic, are you okay?"

"Guess who walked into the night club — two years ago in Los Angeles? Just guess..."

Hayley's eyes were wide. "Magnus?"

I nodded vigorously. "Magnus showed up. He was in normal clothes, and he said he was trying to get to someone, his wife. He gave me a letter to give to his wife if I ever met her. Hayley, he gave me a letter! Oh my god, he's alive. You were right. He's alive. He's not here. He's not in this time. He's stuck in two years ago Los Angeles or something — which is not good, not good at all."

"So where's the letter?"

"Will you come with me to the storage unit?"

"At two in the morning?"

"Hayley, look at me, I'm about to run there on sheer manic excitement, help me. I'm going to burst if I don't go find it."

"Okay sweetie, definitely. I went to bed a lot earlier than anybody should go to bed on a Saturday night, plus, I did not drink enough. Grab some beers for the job. That's a good girl. You driving or me?"

"Me!" I grabbed my bag, the keys, and raced out the door. I came back a second later. "What's taking you so long?"

"I have to pee! The letter's been in a box for two years, it will still be there—"

"Oh my god, oh my god, oh my god, come on Hayley this is too — Magnus is alive!"

CHAPTER 37

*T*wenty minutes later I was sliding the garage door up on my storage unit. Thankfully it was twenty-four-hour access. I wanted to kiss my mom, but then again — I was faced with fifty boxes, no order, no labels, no logic,

Hayley and I forgot to bring something to cut tape, so I used my keys marveling at their many different uses in the past few days. That jerk's DNA was probably still on them from where I swiped at his neck.

Just before Magnus beat him and got away. Magnus got away!

But also, Magnus got away and now he had a vessel and didn't know how to use it. I sliced across the top of a box and dug through the contents: towels, shoes, a bowl of potpourri from the upstairs hallway.

Another box contained some of Lady Mairead's clothing and books from a shelf in the upstairs hallway.

"Got anything, Hayley?"

"A box full of dishes with two desk planners. I'm going through the pages. Who packed like this?"

"I don't know. It's like the person was pissed off at me, but more likely total incompetence."

"She didn't hire them through me. This box has pens and a tape dispenser, spatulas, plus a blank photo album."

"I was going to put wedding photos in there but got side-tracked—" My phone vibrated in my pocket. "It's Zach."

As soon as I answered he started talking. "I just got off work. I'm headed south to pick up Emma, but I just had the weirdest thing happen to me. I have a full memory of something that wasn't there earlier today. It just appeared. It's fucking so crazy Katie—"

"I just had one too. Magnus came to see me about two years ago in Los Angeles. He gave me a letter. I'm in my storage unit trying to find it."

"I helped him find you."

"What?" I stood still running it through my head.

"Two years ago, a man named Magnus, wearing a kilt and carrying a sword, came into the restaurant I was working in and told me this whole story about how he needed help getting to the girl he loved, in Los Angeles. Emma was sitting at the bar, waiting for me to get off work, and she bought the whole story, hook, line, and sinker, because she's a total sucker for romance. He gave us some gold pieces and we helped him buy new clothes. I explained how to use a taxi in the city. And it was you. I wouldn't give him your home address, but I followed you on Twitter. He was going to go to the club there. I don't know how the hell he convinced me. Should have been more cynical about it, but somehow I believed him. I'm sure I've got the gold prob-ably at home in a box. I'm expected in Gainesville so I can't look—"

"Zach thank you, thank you so much. He's so lucky. I'm so lucky that you're in our life, thank you. Drive safe, tell Emma thank you for being a romantic."

"Welcome, I'll see you around three, and we'll move us all back into the house."

I hung up and Hayley stopped sifting through the contents of a box. "Zach has a memory too?"

"Yep, he's how Magnus found me in Los Angeles."

"That's amazing." She ripped open another box.

It was getting tight in the room. We were moving the top boxes off the pile and making one layer all over the floor. It made it hard to move around. "Okay, we're taking a quick break. We both need a beer, a bathroom break, plus we need to create a pile over here of the boxes we've already opened."

Ten minutes later we were back at it. The pile in the middle had dwindled smaller than the pile on the side. Each box had the potential to be 'the box,' but it was disheartening to see the pile get so small, like I was running out of time.

Time for what though? This was an unprecedented thing. It meant everything and nothing — Magnus was alive and looking for me, but we were in the wrong place and times. It was unfathomable how we would get back together. *Zach helped him learn how to take a taxi.*

I pulled open a box. Coffee mugs, a bath mat, a dried flower arrangement, and three books. I pushed it on to the pile of Sifted Through Already.

Then Hayley yelled, "I've got panties!"

I raced to her side and we peered in: a layer of underwear, jewelry, a makeup mirror, and at the bottom, in a pile of belts — the red envelope.

I pulled it out. My hands shook so much I thought I might drop it. I flipped it over and there was the now faded front. The edges were creased and worn. The handwriting though — Magnus's:

Madame Magnus Campbell.

I sat on the floor and clutched it to my chest tears rolling down my cheeks. "He sent me a letter through time."

Hayley said gently, "Would you like to open it?"

I nodded.

I wiped my tears on my wrists and shoved the flyaway hairs from my face. I had been wearing this bun since yesterday morning. I was a wreck. I also wiped some snot from my nose on the closest piece of fabric, a silk scarf from back in my LA days. I didn't want to wet the envelope.

When I decided I would be calm enough to handle it, I inserted a finger under the corner of the sealed flap and tore it up.

Inside was a piece of paper, folded small to fit the square envelope. I gingerly pulled it free. and unfolded it with my eyes closed.

Mo ghradh,

I am alive. Thank ye for doing as I asked. That you are home, safe, waiting, is keeping me alive, able to do this.

The numbers we have used for our vessels no longer work. I am journeying to you, but my time and your time winna coincide. I canna understand the pattern. I am tryin' tae make sense of it by journeyin', but I have tae rest in between and recover my strength. I will nae give up until I am home.

I am coming to you.

I love you, mo reul-iuil,

Magnus

Hayley crouched beside me. "He's coming?"

I nodded, lips clamped between my teeth, holding back a sob.

"This is good sweetie; it's really good."

I nodded again. I folded the paper back, exactly as he had

folded it two years ago and stuffed it into the envelope and clutched it to my chest.

"Are you ready to go back, get some sleep?"

I nodded again.

She gave me a hand and helped me up. "Zach will move in tomorrow. You'll have Emma to fuss over. I'll visit every day, and you'll wait. You can do this right?"

I nodded again.

She said, "Right?"

I straightened my back. "I can do this. He's alive Hayley, he's coming home."

CHAPTER 38

The following months were filled with activity; moving back into my house. Unpacking and organizing. I took ownership more fully, did some redecorating. I left everything that belonged to Lady Mairead in storage and gave the bigger upstairs bedroom to Emma and Zach. It was a melancholy day when I folded Magnus's clothes and placed them in his drawers. It was an exhilarating day when I gave Lady Mairead's room to Zach.

Emma had a nicely rounded tummy. The baby was coming and gave us all something to think about, to focus on, which was helpful when I was bored and lonely. Zach and Emma's room was so large they turned the end of it into a nursery with a rocking chair and a changing table. The downstairs end tables were covered in books about birth and parenting.

I hired a lawyer to get Quentin out of jail, but there wasn't any help for it, he had to finish out the four weeks. But with my promise of a job when he got out, and my lawyer's finagling, he got to keep his gun license so he could actually perform the duties we hired him for. I apologized profusely for not being there when he needed the lawyer, but he simply said, "Ain't no big deal. My own dumb ass for the fight, my own dumb ass for not doing my probation right." He was going to be in a twelve-step program when he got out which he was, "cool with."

I got my parents in line, forced them to believe I was in charge, and assigned Zach and Emma as administrators — just in case. I focused on growing my investments and came up with an amazing idea: I would buy an apartment building. I was thinking James would be the contractor and after it was renovated, Quentin would be the manager. He had the skill-set, and it would give him something to do while there was nothing to do.

Because there wasn't much to do.

Except wait.

Funny how Magnus was the energetic force of our family, the core principle, and without him we were all going through the motions. Zach planned meals. Quentin planned strategies. I created a home base.

Emma waited for the baby.

Waiting.

My days were busy enough. My social life was full though my heart pined. And nights were long. Every night I wished that maybe I would go to sleep and wake up with another memory, but so far there was nothing. Nothing at all.

I read the letter from Magnus over and over again.

CHAPTER 39

I had to go see my grandmother. Mom and Dad and I talked it out. I needed to fly up and see how she was doing, check in on her nurses, and make a plan about where she would live. Dad had her on the waiting list at a home in Orono, but until there was room she had a daily nurse who took care of her a few hours a day. The nurse reported that my grandmother was not doing well. Her memory was worsening; she was losing her ability to remember anything, and I knew it was time. I had to go.

I flew up for the weekend, promising myself that soon I would go for longer. Once Magnus was back. Zach and Quentin knew the drill, they would call me if Magnus arrived. And he would understand. I knew it, but it was still hard to leave.

❧

My grandparents had lived in this house, in town, for as long as I could remember.

"Grandma?" I knocked and pushed open the front door. "Are you home? It's me, Katie, your granddaughter."

My grandmother came around the corner from the kitchen wiping her hands on an apron, squinting at the front door. "Now who on earth is it there?"

"It's me, Katie." She looked at me blankly. "Kaitlyn Sheffield, John's daughter, your grand daughter?"

"Ah!" She said like that explained it, then looked confused again. "Katie is a little girl, you can't be Katie..." Her face fell with worry.

"But I am Grandma. It's me, Katie. You just haven't seen me in a while because I've been in California. Now I live down the street from your son, John." I walked in and put my overnight bag by the couch. Smoke wafted out of the kitchen. "Is Marsha here, are you baking?"

Grandma looked down, wringing her hands.

I implemented Steamroller Protocol: barge in, take over, repeat who I was, and continuously tell her it was okay. "Everything's cool Grandma. It's me, Katie. Are you cooking something?"

I stalked past her. Smoke billowed out of the oven. I located oven mitts and extracted a tray of what looked like it was once cheese toast, but was now charcoal. It could have been a fire. "You're cooking. When I used to visit you in the summers we loved to cook together. Do you remember Grandma? We cooked elaborate experimental meals. Me and you, little Katie and her grandma. Cooking."

"Little Katie loved cooking."

"Yes, I do. I love to cook. And I love visiting my grandma Barb." I scrolled through my contacts and found Marsha's phone number and called it.

She answered, "Hello?"

"Hi Marsha, it's Katie Sheffield. I'm here at Barb's house, and um, she's just burned a tray of cheese toast."

Marsha's voice said, "She's not allowed to cook if I'm not there."

"Yeah, of course, um what time are you coming today?"

"Today I don't come until three."

It was eleven. The house would have been burned down by then or who knows what. "Okay, I'll see you at three." I hung up.

"So Grandma, me and you, little Katie, your granddaughter and you, Barb, my grandma are going to have a really nice visit this weekend—"

"Katie?"

"Yes!" I rushed to my bag and pulled out a box of photos. "I have photos, would you like to see them? Of me, little Katie?" I cleared a place at the table and put down the box.

My grandmother said, "Little Katie, you have grown up."

"I have, I'm all grown up now. I'm even married."

"Aw, that's wonderful dear."

I pulled out a handful of photos and starting with my childhood showed them to her talking about each one. Eventually she was used to the fact that I was her granddaughter. But then she became confused about where her husband was, and I had to start a whole new kind of steamroll, "Grandpa Jack isn't here anymore. He's with God now. He passed away and went to heaven about four years ago, and you were very sad. And I was very sad. But the ceremony was just lovely and now—"

"Jack is gone..."

"He is Grandma, but you'll see him sometime, in the next life. He's waiting for you."

"Remember that time he got lost at Disney World? We couldn't find him for so long, but then he was sitting right in front of the Lost Child office. He was fifty, but they had given him some ears to wear on his head and a sticker with his name on it?"

"I do, I remember it like it was yesterday. I was five years old at the time."

She giggled. I could see from the sparkle in her eyes that this was a good visual memory. I grabbed another handful of photos and looked through it for scenes from that day. I found one, me and Grandpa holding hands. It was before he had gotten lost. Grandma screwed up her mouth confused. "That's you, Katie, but that's..."

"That's Grandpa, Jack, your husband of fifty-five years. Those are good memories aren't they Grandma?"

She nodded.

"Are you hungry?"

"I am. I could use a bite, would you like me to make you something?"

"I'd like to make you something." I opened the cupboards, which were mostly empty and the fridge which was also mostly empty. My hope was the lack of food was to keep Grandma from making her own meals, but also, what did she eat when no one was here? Would Marsha go by the store on her way here? And why didn't Dad have a plan for this?

Because she was so far away; it was easy to forget she needed us.

There was some bread and more cheese, so I made some new cheese toast. I slid it under the broiler for a minute then placed it in front of her.

"Thank you, dear." She ate happily and then grinned. "You remind me a lot of my Katie."

"I am Katie."

"Of course, that makes perfect sense." She chewed another bite. "Show me more of your photos."

"Sure." I showed her photos of me at my high school graduation. One of me wearing my prom dress standing beside James. And a photo of me in my college dorm. None of these made much of an impression. Her memory was so much worse than last time I was here, two long years ago. Steamroller Protocol was entirely different on the phone when I couldn't see how confused she looked.

I sifted through a stack of photos with Braden in them. My Los Angeles years had been all about him. I shoved them to the side to toss in the trash.

"Grandma I wanted to show you photos of my wedding."

She clapped her hands happily. "I love weddings! Have I ever told you about my wedding?"

I stopped mid-search and listened. These moments were too fleeting to not give it my full attention.

"He was home from the Vietnam War and my dress was spectacular, cinched so tight around my waist that it's a wonder I didn't faint away when he said his vows." Her eyes went faraway like she pictured it.

"I thought I was going to faint too, Grandma, during our ceremony. We had our hands tied together. And it was intense and also beautiful."

"That's a Celtic tradition, Handfasting."

"My husband is Scottish. So that's why we did it. And it was beautiful."

"I remember I couldn't look at him. If I looked up I was going to hyperventilate, instead I just looked at my knuckles."

"Me too! I focused on our hands and tried to remember to breathe through it."

My grandmother clasped her hands together. "Oh, it is such a wonderful thing to be married to someone. You will hate him and love him and want to escape him and infuriate him, sometimes all in the same hour, but also, if he is devoted and fair and even-tempered, you've got a good road ahead of you."

"Grandpa was all those things, wasn't he?"

"He was a good man."

"I think my husband is all of those things too. It's still so new, and it's complicated because we're so different. But he's adaptable and has a good spirit."

"That's wonderful dear. Can I see the photos?"

I had put them in the box precisely to show her so I got to them easily and spread them out on the table. The photos of me and Magnus in our wedding clothes on the back deck of our house, on the front steps of the church, and leaned together in front of our decadent wedding feast. I loved that photo so much, how we were together, married, but that lean was one of our first times touching each other. It was as much a promise as our oaths had been hours before. Because it was us, together, now—

"Is that Magnus Cam—" She peered at the photo and another one. "Why it is, it's Magnus Campbell, did you marry our Magnus, Katie?"

I stared at her dumbfounded.

"Such a nice boy. From Scotland. Oh that's right, you said your husband was from Scotland. I might have put the two together—"

"Grandma, how do you know Magnus?"

"He used to live here. Remember back when your grandpa and I would take in the university students? When was that, back in the early nineties, I think? Was that before you were born? It was mostly students from Jack's classes, but then Magnus came along... I'm not sure exactly how we met him, but he stayed here for a couple of months and really became like family. You remember, I'm sure we talked about Magnus before."

My eyes welled up with tears. I shook my head. "I don't remember you ever mentioning him."

"He was like a son, such a sweet boy." She stood and went to her bookcase and ran a finger along a row of photo album spines with tags that said: 1984-86, 1984-graduation, 1987-Europe, etcetera, and pulled one off the shelf and returned with it. She flipped through a few pages and pointed. "There he is, at our lake house, with your grandpa."

I sobbed while smiling looking down on the photo. The photo page was antiqued from time — twenty-five years ago.

My grandpa was young, smiling and waving. The lake behind them. Their bare feet on my family's dock — a place I hadn't seen in years — and Magnus, smiling, tanned, waving, an arm around my grandpa. Grandpa's arm around Magnus. There was so much going on in my heart and mind that I didn't know what to say.

"Why was he here?"

My grandmother was looking at other pages, but it was the only photo of Magnus in the book. "Oh he was an exchange student or something, or—" She looked up at the ceiling. "Funny, the memory is clear as day. He was working on a math equation. He had a bunch of numbers, longitudes and star charts, and was always thinking on it. Jack took him to the university, and he talked to professors there about it. At night we sat around the table with books open, talking and trying to solve it. It was all so much fun. I suppose it was his graduate thesis or something that part is a little hazy now. But it's been twenty-five years, you know."

She leaned back in her chair. Looked at the ceiling for a moment. I was worried she might have questions about Magnus's age, or her memory, or why it was so clear, or anything, but then she returned to my wedding photos. "This is lovely dear. It is so good to see Magnus again. You'll have to bring him here, next trip. I know Jack would love to..." Her voice trailed off and she looked around confused.

I put the photos back in the boxes and returned her photo album to the shelf. I spent the rest of the weekend kind of looking for a note or message though I wasn't sure where one would be. And how would it last for twenty-five years?

I opened up the back of frames and looked on the underside of the guest room furniture, but really — I had my message. Magnus came to my grandparents' house. They helped him work his equations. Grandma thought of him like family. I felt warm inside, happy. He was coming home. It was just a matter of time.

But the warm family feeling about Magnus also felt like a sign. If Magnus was a part of Grandma's family, and mine, shouldn't she be a part of the family again, too? And we all lived in Florida.

So I made a unilateral decision to move her to Amelia Island. I argued it out with Mom and Dad. I packed her suitcase, bought her a ticket, and brought her home on the plane.

She stayed in the guest room newly vacated by Zach and Emma, and by Tuesday she was on a shortlist for a spot at a local assisted-living facility. A moving company would pack up her things and bring them down.

CHAPTER 40

This time could only be described as expansive. Last time Magnus was gone I waited, worried and unsure. In a holding pattern, looping around inside his house, with his staff, in his life. But this time I was truly running a household. I had gathered Magnus's chosen clan around me, and I was caring for all of them. Organizing, managing, making a ton of lists with little check marks down the sides: done, done, done. On enthusiastic days I scratched lines through the entries — finished.

I was Kaitlyn Campbell, and I ran this shit. I was Queen of the Highlander's castle.

I was super proud.

And I never thought about Lady Mairead's threat that I would never see him again.

Mostly.

Days passed, weeks, and then months. So much time that the waiting went from active to passive and then to waiting, but not thinking about it nearly as much. It freaked me out but was probably totally necessary to keep me sane.

Turning off the worrying, thinking, hoping, crying. It was a relief.

I went out. I met Hayley, Michael, and James for drinks. I drank shots and laughed and danced and sparred with James as per usual.

"Alone again Katie?" His face when he teased me like this was incredulous. "You've got to be getting pretty lonely by now."

"Yes and yes and none of your business."

He drank a bit more. "You sure you don't need someone to keep you company?"

"God no, I'm married."

"I've just never known someone to see their husband so little. It almost makes the whole marriage thing seem like a sham. Ya sure you ain't bullshitting us?"

"Nope. Magnus just has work. Scotland work. . . "

"I know what you told me he does. I know what you said, but here's what it looks like: You're a newlywed. You've been married for almost a year. You went and spent four months alone in a 'hippy camp' and you've seen your husband for all of a — how long?"

"Like a week. . . "

"See, I don't want to be the one that tells you this, but seriously Katie, he's gone." He dropped his voice, "and whatever bullshit story he told you about where he is, well that's on you for believing him."

"Bullshit."

"Not from where I'm sitting." He leaned back, hands out. "Hey, I'm the kind of guy who would do that if I could. You know me, I'm not faulting a man for trying to get a bit on the side. It's what men do, but I just thought you were smarter."

Hayley came back from the bathroom and looked at our faces. "Miss anything?"

"James is insinuating that Magnus left me, that all men play around, and that I'm a dumbass for waiting for him."

"Michael are you going to sit there and let him say shit like that to Katie? You need to step up."

"What am I going to say? He's making some good points."

"He said all men play around, you playing around? You agree with him? Because I'm walking if you don't distance yourself from this right now."

Michael said, "Big J is full of shit."

"Exactly. Magnus just has business. That's all it is. He'll be back soon. And James you shut up. You sound like a dick. And a loser. "

James held up his hand in his I'm-a-dick-but-mostly charming kind of way. "I was just calling it like I see it, no hard feelings, right Katie?"

"No hard feelings. But seriously James, you keep arguing that all men are lying cheaters and you're going to believe it. And then you'll become one of those guys who can't perform because you're so shallow and empty and small and lonely. I think you should try to be better than that."

"Ouch."

"Yep, ouch."

"Let me buy you a drink, and we'll talk about something more fun."

"No hitting on me anymore though, I'm married. My husband carries a sword. Plus, I was going to offer you a job."

"A job?"

"I need a contractor for some apartments I'm buying."

Because life had to go on. There was a future to think of. People to care for and worry about, in the here and now.

Also the future.

There was a baby about to be born. A bestie about to be married. Work to be done.

And so that's what I would do, be Kaitlyn, forward-thinking, future-planner.

And so that's what I did.

For months.

CHAPTER 41

he side of the bed shifted slightly. "Huh?" I woke from deep sleep to a full start. "What?" The room was dark, there was someone sitting on the side of the bed their back to me —

Magnus's voice whispered, "Tis me Kaitlyn."

His voice rumbled through my heart, vibrating in my nerves.

"Magnus?" I was fuzzy-headed, confused.

His sword slid along the ground under the bed, a familiar sound.

One of his shoes hit the ground.

"You're home?" My confused, sleep-addled brain couldn't believe it was true. It was too dark to see him fully.

"Aye. Tis quite painful — Quentin helped me up the board-walk." He pulled off his other shoe with a groan. He climbed into bed and pulled up tight against me, on my arm, nestling his face into me, his arm across my stomach, a heavy leg on my legs.

I said, "It's really you?"

"Aye." His breath was warm on my chest.

"Okay." I kissed his forehead.

He sat quietly. His breath growing long and deep, and his body growing heavy. Then he asked, "What is that sound?"

"It's Zach and Emma's baby,"

His scratchy face rubbed heavy on my shoulder when he said, "Good. I'm home, thank ye, but I have to sleep…"

"Of course." I pressed my lips to his forehead again and hugged his shoulders. "Good night, Magnus." His face nestled in deeper to my side and a moment later he was fast asleep.

CHAPTER 42

$\mathcal{I}$ couldn't help it, when he woke up I was sitting over him breathless with excitement. "Hi."

"Good mornin', mo reul-iuil."

"You're home. I can't believe it. You're really home. I mean, I knew you were trying, but you actually did it."

"I canna believe it either, though it took enough pain of me. I am verra glad tae be."

I bounced on the bed. Looking him in the eyes, not wanting the moment, him, waking up, home, *finally* — to ever end.

"I'm literally so excited I don't think I slept for the last four hours."

"What time is it? What day?"

"It's June 10th." I glanced over at the clock on the side table. "Six-forty-five."

"I have the grime of centuries on me, want tae take a shower?"

"God, yes."

I energetically jumped from the bed and bounded across the

room. I looked back and Magnus was smiling. "What are you waiting for?"

"I am nae waiting, I am watching. Your arse in your panties leaping across the room. Tis quite spectacular."

I grinned. "In one half second it will be — wait, right now." I dropped my panties to the ground, wiggled my butt cheeks at him, and ran into the bathroom giggling. Magnus, my Magnus, jumped from bed and followed a step behind.

I started the shower while he stripped his clothes to the floor. Steamy hot. I pulled my shirt off over my head, tossed it to the side, and then led him by the hand into our shower. He held his breath, ducked into the water, said, "phwesha!" and shook like a dog, sprinkling water around the stall.

I filled my hand with shampoo, and he dutifully leaned forward. I scrubbed his hair massaging in circles as he groaned.

"When did ye know I was coming home?"

"I had been back for a day. I was sleeping on the couch. Hayley was here, because long story, and I woke up and had a new memory, you, in Los Angeles."

"It worked then? Did ye keep it that long?"

"Yes it worked. I did. I can't explain why, but I kept it."

I took the handle off the shower wall and sprayed his head. Soap bubbles poured down his skin. He asked, "What did ye think of me in Los Angeles?"

"I thought you were hot and mysterious. What did you think of Los Angeles me?"

"I thought ye were the most beautiful thing I had ever seen. I also thought I might shove a knife point into the man ye were with and save ye the trouble, but I believed ye might nae fall in love with me after."

"I'm super glad you had second thoughts."

"Me too, mo reul-iuil." He tipped up my chin and looked down into my eyes. "You ran because I told ye tae."

"I did, I ran."

"Twas the first time I thought we might survive these travails. I have been thinking on this for many a day. If ye trusted me tae do it against your own strong will, I had tae be smart and keep journeyin' tae get home. It made me think afore I shoved knives intae scoundrels."

I lathered soap all over his shoulders. "So I was like your North Star?"

"Och aye."

"Turn around." I lathered his back. The whip marks were healed mostly, becoming stripes of scars. Most of them ugly, a few of them very, very ugly. I kissed one and lathered under his arms and down his waist and around his buttocks.

"I dinna think I could love ye more but when ye hit Lord Delapointe and ran, I was verra proud of ye. It made me know, truly know, that ye were everything tae me. As if I found ye on purpose because we were meant tae be."

I pushed his shoulder, so he turned to face me. "If you keep talking like that you'll make me cry, and there has been too much of that. We are having a happy shower. No tears, either happy or sad."

"Still, I was verra proud, needed tae be said," He grinned and lathered soap on my breasts.

I moaned. "Good, I'm glad that moment was an epiphany for you, because I don't know if I could ever do it again. Leaving you took all the strength I have. I don't want to do that anymore."

His strong hands pulled me close to his front and then without much ceremony at all he set his stance firm and lifted me from the ground. But I climbed him too, wrapping my legs around his waist. I held onto his steaming wet shoulders. And because it had been too long, too, too long — he was inside me fast, and around me, desperate and fast and with oh so much desperate longing and quick because it needed to happen

quickly, at once. Now. Because oh my god, it had been so long. .
.

I held on around his shoulders. Slippery shoulders — "don't drop me" — His breath beside my ear. "I winna let go" — wide and strong and hard and — I pressed my nose to his shoulder and inhaled the scent of him mingled with the water — my back pushed to the glass. His hips slamming against mine. Steam surrounding us. Shampoo scents lingering in the air. My moans against his wet skin.

In the end he slid from inside me as I slid from his hands down his front to my feet. I landed, and wrapped my arms around his chest and tucked my head there. His arms around. He kissed the edge of my hair, inhaled and his arms went tighter. I held on. I pressed against him like my life depended on it. And felt him solid, alive, real.

Steam rose all around us and many long moments passed. I wouldn't let go. He wouldn't. It was a promise, and the longer we held the more it meant. Finally another kiss to my forehead and we broke our embrace.

He scrubbed his hands up and down on his face and grinned. "You told me once it was uncomfortable tae do in a shower. I think the end result may be worth the difficulties."

I lathered up my hair. "True. We could also install a seat that would make it less acrobatic?"

"But then ye winna have tae climb me."

I raised the shower handle to rinse my hair and grinned. "You liked that, huh?"

"I did."

"Good, me too."

He kissed me on the nose. "I am hungry enough tae eat a bear. What magic has Chef Zach whipped up, ye think?"

"Probably pancakes or something. I heard him up early. It must be something special."

"Tis all special when I am half-starved. He has a bairn?"

"Yes, a boy. He and Emma named him Ben. He's three weeks old."

"Tis a full house when a bairn is in residence."

"Also, my grandma, Barbara—"

"Madame Barb is here?"

"She is, I brought her—"

"Och aye, tis good news. . . "

I smiled broadly. "There aren't many men who would be thrilled by the idea of a grandmother moving into their house."

"Are ye telling me one of your jokes? Madame Barb is wonderful. When I lived there, I understood where ye got your wit. She would banter with a spark in her eye much like your own. Twas hard tae believe I would ever get tae see ye again — you hadna been born yet, but being around Madame Barbara was comfortable, like being home with ye. She is so wise about — you are joking?"

I watched him for a beat, my heart soaring from the sight of him, the sound of his words, the feel of his hands. "You know — yes, she's here. I applied to get her in an assisted-living home, and she's moving there on Monday. You can help us move her."

"Tis close?"

"Just down the street."

"Good."

"Her memory is terrible, but she remembers you really well."

"Like twas yesterday." He grinned, finished toweling off, and left for the bedroom to put on clothes while I finished my shower. A moment later he stuck his head back into the bathroom. "Tis waffles, mo reul-iuil. Chef Zach has declared them ready."

~

The End of Book Two. . .

THANK YOU

This is not the true end of Magnus and Kaitlyn. There will be more chapters in their story.

Thank you for taking the time to read this book. The world is full of entertainment and I appreciate that you chose to spend some time with Magnus and Kaitlyn. I fell in love with Magnus when I was writing him, and I hope you fell in love a little bit too.

Please leave a review. I'm writing the next installment and I love the encouragement.

Review Time and Space Between Us

If you need help getting through the pauses before the next books, there is a FB group here: Kaitlyn and the Highlander, now at over 3,000 fans.

Kaitlyn and the Highlander (Book 1)
Time and Space Between Us (Book 2)
Warrior of My Own (Book 3)
Begin Where We Are (Book 4)
A Missing Entanglement (now a prologue within book 5)
Entangled with You (Book 5)
Magnus and a Love Beyond Words (Book 6)
Under the Same Sky (book 7)
Nothing But Dust (book 8)
Again My Love (book 9)
Our Shared Horizon (book 10)
Son and Throne (coming soon)

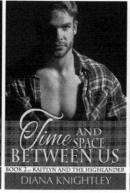
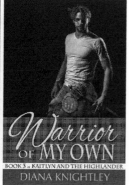

SERIES ORDER

Kaitlyn and the Highlander (Book 1)
Time and Space Between Us (Book 2)
Warrior of My Own (Book 3)
Begin Where We Are (Book 4)
A Missing Entanglement (now a prologue within book 5)
Entangled with You (Book 5)
Magnus and a Love Beyond Words (Book 6)
Under the Same Sky (book 7)
Nothing But Dust (book 8)
Again My Love (book 9)
Our Shared Horizon (book 10)
Son and Throne (coming soon)

Can he see to the depths of her mystery before it's too late?

The oceans cover everything, the apocalypse is behind them. Before them is just water, leveling. And in the middle — they find each other.

On a desolate, military-run Outpost, Beckett is waiting.

Then Luna bumps her paddleboard up to the glass windows and disrupts his everything.

And soon Beckett has something and someone to live for. Finally. But their survival depends on discovering what she's hiding, what she won't tell him.

Because some things are too painful to speak out loud.

With the clock ticking, the water rising, and the storms growing, hang on while Beckett and Luna desperately try to rescue each other in Leveling, the epic, steamy, and suspenseful first book of the trilogy, Luna's Story:

Leveling: Book One of Luna's Story

Under: Book Two of Luna's Story

Deep: Book Three of Luna's Story

SOME THOUGHTS AND RESEARCH...

Some **Scottish and Gaelic words** that appear within the books:

Turadh - a break in the clouds between showers

Solasta - luminous shining (possible nickname)

Splang - flash, spark, sparkle

Dreich - dull and miserable weather

Mo reul-iuil - my North Star (nickname)

Tha thu a 'fàileadh mar ghaoith - you have the scent of a breeze.

Osna - a sigh

Rionnag - star

Sollier - bright

Ghrian - the sun

Mo ghradh - my own love

Tha thu breagha - you are beautiful

Mo chroi - my heart

Corrachag-cagail - dancing and flickering ember flames

Mo reul-iuil, is ann leatsa abhios mo chridhe gubrath - My North Star, my heart belongs to you forever

Dinna ken - didn't know

~

Characters:

Kaitlyn Maude Sheffield

Magnus Archibald Caelhin Campbell

Lady Mairead (Campbell) Delapointe

John Sheffield (Kaitlyn's father)

Paige Sheffield (Kaitlyn's Mother)

James Cook

Quentin Peters

Zach Greene

Emma Garcia

Michael Greene

Hayley Sherman

The Earl of Breadalbane

Uncle Archibald (Baldie) Campbell

~

Locations:

Fernandina Beach on Amelia Island, Florida, 2017

Magnus's castle - Balloch. Built in 1552. In early 1800s it was rebuilt as Taymouth Castle. Situated on the south bank of the River Tay, in the heart of the Grampian Mountains

~

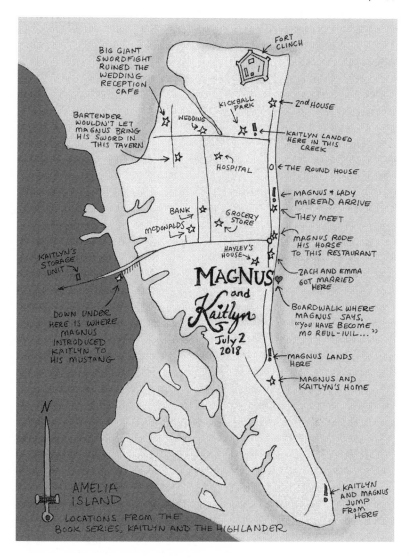

ACKNOWLEDGMENTS

My Facebook page was kicking it for a while there. My friends and family weighed in on many questions I had about how Magnus would find the new New World. The conversation continued over in the FB group, Kaitlyn and the Highlander. My readers there answered even more questions for me, like "Were kilts too cold for a Scottish winter?"

Thank you to Anne Leyden for mentioning that Magnus would be impressed by bandaids (These play a big role in book 2, helping Kaitlyn escape Delapointe.)

Thank you to Jessica Fox for reading and advising. You also asked what Zach was cooking for breakfast when Magnus returned and so I added the line: A moment later he stuck his head back into the bathroom. "Tis waffles, mo reul-iuil. Chef Zach has declared them ready."

To Heather Hawkes for reading and texting and yelling and feeling and expressing about all that Kaitlyn goes through in the 18th century. You felt it deeply and I knew then you loved the characters and I appreciate that just so so so much.

And to D. Thompson who has been reading ARCs for me,

book after book after book, and was asked so many questions this time — you helped me with your kind words, "Just write, don't second guess." Thank you.

Thank you to Kevin Dowdee for being my support, my guidance, and my inspiration for these stories. I appreciate you so much. And thank you for revisiting Scotland with me on our honeymoon. That was awesome.

Thank you to my kids, Ean, Gwynnie, Fiona, and Isobel, for listening to me go on and on about these characters and accepting them as real parts of our lives. When I asked, "Guess what Magnus's favorite flavor of ice cream is?" They answered, "Vanilla," without blinking an eye. Also, when I asked, "What is Magnus's favorite band?" They answered, "Foo Fighters." (necessary in book 2) So yeah, thank you for thinking of my book characters like a part of our family.

And a huge thank you to Isobel Dowdee for putting your care and attention to the pages. Your suggestions, advice, knowledge, and opinions are always so amazing. I'm blown away by how you make the story better and better.

ABOUT ME, DIANA KNIGHTLEY

I live in Los Angeles where we have a lot of apocalyptic tendencies that we overcome by wishful thinking. Also great beaches. I maintain a lot of people in a small house, too many pets, and a to-do list that is longer than it should be, because my main rule is: Art, play, fun, before housework. My kids say I am a cool mom because I try to be kind. I'm married to a guy who is like a water god, he surfs, he paddle boards, he built a boat. I'm a huge fan.

I write about heroes and tragedies and magical whisperings and always forever happily ever afters. I love that scene where the two are desperate to be together but can't because of war or apocalyptic-stuff or (scientifically sound!) time-jumping and he is begging the universe with a plead in his heart and she is distraught (yet still strong) and somehow, through kisses and steamy more and hope and heaps and piles of true love, they manage to come out on the other side.

I like a man in a kilt, especially if he looks like a Hemsworth, doesn't matter, Liam or Chris.

My couples so far include Beckett and Luna (from the trilogy, Luna's Story). Who battle their fear to find each other during an apocalypse of rising waters. And, coming soon, Magnus and Kaitlyn (from the series Kaitlyn and the Highlander). Who find themselves traveling through time and space to be together.

I write under two pen names, this one here, Diana Knightley, and another one, H. D. Knightley, where I write books for Young

Adults. (They are still romantic and fun and sometimes steamy though, because love is grand at any age.)

DianaKnightley.com
Diana@dianaknightley.com

ALSO BY H. D. KNIGHTLEY (MY YA PEN NAME)

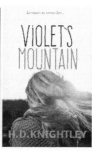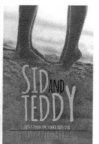

Bright (Book One of The Estelle Series)

Beyond (Book Two of The Estelle Series)

Belief (Book Three of The Estelle Series)

Fly; The Light Princess Retold

Violet's Mountain

Sid and Teddy

Made in the USA
Middletown, DE
21 November 2020